THE DOWNSTAIRS TENANT

AND OTHER STORIES

ACKNOWLEDGMENTS

Special thanks to my mother, Joyce Parsley, and, as always, to Greg Bachmeier. Also special acknowledgement to Phyllis Barber, Chris Noel and Benet Tvedten, OSB.

Some of the stories in *The Downstairs Tenant* were published in a different form in the following places:

"LeeLand Franken's Bible" won second place in the 1994 *Wellspring* Short Fiction Contest.

"Earth" and "Hush" originally were published in *Thunder Sandwich*.

"Jesús' Ashes" first appeared in *Steam Ticket*.

"Ita's Baby" first was published in *Burning Light*.

"The Letter" originally was published in *The Lawrence Review*.

"Mrs. Wentworth's Azaleas" first appeared in *HallowMass*.

"Munda Cor Meum" originally was published (in a different form) in the anthology *Mondo Barbie II*.

"Magenta" originally was published in *Quietist*.

"The Bishop Comes For a Visit" originally was produced in December 1996 at the Shield Theater.

ALSO BY JAMIE PARSLEY

Paper Doves, Falling and Other Poems (1992)

The Loneliness of Blizzards (1995)

Cloud (1997)

The Wounded Table (1999)

earth into earth, water into water (2000)

Ikon (2005)

Just Once (2007)

This Grass (2009)

Fargo, 1957 (2010)

Crow (2012)

That Word (2014)

THE DOWNSTAIRS TENANT

And Other Stories by

JAMIE PARSLEY

Published by the Institute for Regional Studies Press
North Dakota State University
Dept. 2360, P.O. Box 6050, Fargo, ND 58108-6050.
www.ndsu.edu/ahss/ndirs

The Downstairs Tenant
By Jamie Parsley

Copyright ©2014 by the Institute for Regional Studies Press, North Dakota State University, Fargo. All rights reserved.

Cover image courtesy NDSU Archives, Fargo (2006.7.4)
Book design by Deb Tanner.

International Standard Book Number: 978-0-911042-80-1
Library of Congress Control Number: 2014957688
Printed in the United States.

In memory:

JEFFREY "J.D." GOULD
June 13, 1956 – July 29, 2013

What green-eyed girl
have you left behind?

She waits for you—
love-sick and broken.

As we all are.
She lies there

on the porch steps
waiting for you.

She will wait.
As we all will.

CONTENTS

1. "AND THE MORNING STARS SANG..." 1

    The Downstairs Tenant 3
    Ita's Baby 9
    LeeLand Franken's Bible 27
    The Letter 37
    Mrs. Wentworth's Azaleas 49
    Munda Cor Meum 63
    From Amidst the Wind 71
    "I Could've Gone On Forever" 83

2. A COLD, COMFORTING SILENCE 101

    Jesús' Ashes 103
    Hush 107
    This 111
    Earth 123
    Burying the Ashes 135
    Magenta 141

3. THE BISHOP COMES FOR A VISIT (a play) 147

"Beauty is everlasting
and dust is for a time."

— Marianne Moore

INTRODUCTION

The catalyst for me to collect these stories was a car accident. In the summer of 2012, I was a passenger in a car that was sideswiped. I ended up fracturing two vertebrae, a rib and, inexplicably, I also fractured a tooth. The accident came at an inopportune time in my life: I had just quit a job I had greatly enjoyed under difficult and unfortunate circumstances. And I was in the end stages of mourning deeply for my father almost two years after his very sudden death.

In the long months of recovery after the accident, I found myself, for the first time in my writing career, without a project. I had just published my eleventh book of poems, *Crow*. My tenth book of poems, *Fargo, 1957*, published a year and half before, was garnering much attention at that time and was selling better than any of my previous books. But I was feeling compelled to do something else with my next project. After unsuccessfully attempting one or two nonfiction pieces and briefly considering adapting *Fargo, 1957* into a play (which I actually just recently completed), one very hot afternoon, while going through a plastic bin of old manuscripts, I came across a discarded script of a short fiction collection. The ten or so stories in the manuscript were written from a period in the late 1980s through 1990s. These stories, and the stories I wrote following my discovery, helped me through my convalescence.

The stories are stories of Dakota in the mid-twentieth century. For the better part of my life, this period in United States history has intrigued and, at times, obsessed me. Most of the earliest stories I heard were stories that often took place against the backdrop of this time in history, and so it is only natural that these stories, too, happened to fall within that time frame.

At some point in collecting the stories and sending them out to select writer friends to critique, I was made aware that many of the main characters (and, in some cases, the pivotal characters) were women. There was certainly nothing intentional in this, nor was there anything intentional in the fact that many of them came across, at times, as harsh or unforgiving. Still, as I pondered (and, at times, fretted over) this, I also came to realize that most of the earliest stories I heard in my own life were told to me by women about women (usually by my mother, my aunt or my maternal grandmother). Oftentimes, the women in those stories (and the women telling me those stories) were also, at times, brash. I feared, as I churned over this, that my attempt to capture strong, independent women might seem unfair or negative to women in general. At some point, I brought this issue to my mother, who also faithfully read the stories through their various revisions. My mother's response was telling: "Anyone who thinks women back then were too hard or too bitchy obviously didn't live then. Oftentimes, our hardness and brashness was what helped us stay strong when life seemed unfairly turned against us. Sometimes you just had to be tough or hard or strong as a woman at that time."

One writer friend of mine, when I asked her point-blank if I was too harsh in these characters, laughed at me. "I'm just happy you didn't present them as submissive, vain, frivolous or spineless. I wouldn't have been able to stomach that. Nor would I have been able to forgive you as a writer." She added, "Most of your characters—whether male or female—are appropriately grotesque at turns. On that account, you are equal in your opportunities to reveal their malformations."

Five of the stories included here are "retellings" of the *Palm-of-the-Hand Stories* of Yasunari Kawabata. While in graduate school, pursuing a Master of Fine Arts degree in both poetry and fiction, I discovered Kawabata's haikulike stories. They amazed and delighted me in a way few discoveries had before them. They came into my life like a lightning bolt that set everything aflame.

Kawabata (1882-1972) was a brilliant writer and was the first Japanese winner of the Nobel Prize for Literature (in 1968). Primarily a novelist (author of such classic Japanese novels as *The Dancing Girl of Izo*, *Snow Country*, *The Master of Go* and *The House of the Sleeping Beauties*), he wrote his *Palm-of-the-Hand Stories* throughout the 1920s and 1930s.

Probably one of the more interesting aspects of Kawabata's life was his intense aloneness. By the age of eight, he had lost both of his parents and his sister. By sixteen, he had lost the grandfather who took care of him. He had lost so many relatives by the time he turned twenty that he earned the nickname "the master of funerals." Certainly I was drawn to his sense of aloneness. It permeated almost every word of his writing.

Initially, Kawabata had hoped to be a painter. Because of this interest, he cultivated an "artist's eye." This gift not only made him a keen observer of nature, but of people. There is no doubt that his artist's eye found its perfection in the fiction he wrote. This, coupled with his aloneness, made his stories even more unique and precise.

As I encountered the *Palm-of-the-Hand Stories*, I found them perplexing, daunting, exhilarating and stunning. I wanted to delve deeper and deeper into them at times. I found the best way to do so for me, as a reader of the stories who also happens to be a writer, came in the form of taking the general plots of the stories and "retelling" them in American (or, more specifically, in American Upper Midwestern) terms. In doing so, I was able to approach Kawabata and his writing not as a critic interested in what his work meant, but as a writer interested in the intricacies, the depths and layers of his work.

I use the term "retell" rather than the word "adapt." Adapt was a term that I initially used, which seemed to imply more than what I was intending to do in these stories. It seemed too scholarly a word. It almost conveyed a sense of translation when, in reality, I had no intention of "translating" them, nor was I interested in simply writing an "American transparency" of these thoroughly Japanese stories. My intention, as a writer and, more specifically as a storyteller, was to retell the story in much the same way John Sturges' *The Magnificent Seven* is a retelling of Akira Kurosawa's *Seven Samurai* or, in turn, as Kurosawa's *Rain* is a retelling of the King Lear story.

I also kept in mind as I wrote them some of what the American poet H.D. (1887-1961) did with ancient Greek texts. H.D. in no way claimed to be "translating" the work. She took already existing texts, translated by others into English, and rewrote them in her own superbly "Imagist" style.

Keeping these examples in mind, I cautiously tackled these *Palm-of-the-Hand Stories* and, after wrestling with them and delving deeper into them, I was (I hope) able to truly get to the heart and guts of them. I must repeat, though: In writing them, I was cautious. I felt at times as though I was trampling through sacred ground, possibly destroying and dirtying the purity of Kawabata's work.

When I was finished, my appreciation of and respect for Kawabata and his characters was more defined. I experienced through these retellings the personal pain, loneliness and loss (the three real pillars of his stories, I believe) on a very intimate level. Kawabata, the man, the lover, the son and grandson, the child-master of funerals, was not only present in these stories as observer, but was present in his own characters. Those aspects in myself also were confronted and embraced.

Probably the one aspect I related to the most in Kawabata and his stories was his role as the perpetual observer. Kawabata's stories are not autobiography. In fact, one would be hard-pressed to find any of the writer's personal life in any of his stories. That has been an important aspect of my own life as a writer as well, especially concerning my fiction. The role of the perpetual observer allows one a perspective that is always fresh and unique — dare I say, a feeling of omnipotence. But, there is a price to pay for such a perspective. With it comes a sense of aloneness. More often, Kawabata is not in the inside looking out. Rather, he is on the outside looking in. For some, this might be a curse. For a writer like Kawabata, it is essential.

I consider myself fortunate to have had Kawabata affect me as he did. As a writer, I have been able to stand back from my own work and re-examine it in the sometimes glaring light of what he did. In a very real sense, reading and re-telling Kawabata has revolutionized my own writing. Certainly everything I held to be vital to understanding what a story was before I encountered the *Palm-of-the-Hand Stories* changed drastically. Kawabata helped me bridge my training as a poet with my love of writing fiction. Through his stories, I came to realize that I could write short fiction using many of the techniques I learned as a poet. Robert Penn Warren, who also wrote both poetry and fiction, once said, "Poetry is the great schoolhouse of fiction." Still, Kawabata himself was not a poet — at least, he never considered himself one. In fact, he once said,

> "Many writers, in their youth, write poetry: I, instead of poetry, wrote the palm-of-the-hand stories ... the poetic spirit of my young days lives on in them." (Editorial note. *Palm-of-the-Hand Stories* (translated by Lane Dunlop and J. Martin Holman).

Finally, this collection ends with what might seem a departure from the rest of the book—a play. Although I debated whether or not I should include it here, "The Bishop Comes For a Visit," is, I believe, not such a departure as one might initially think. In many ways, the play, telling a story in much the same way fiction tells a story, fits well into the ebb and flow of this book. It, like the stories that precede it, carries with it a subtle sense of aloneness and a tinge of darkness. Of course, the period of time it portrays also fits into the rest of the book. It is also unique for another reason: Unlike the other stories in this collection, the play actually is based very loosely on an actual story I heard while working in a church parish in a small rural community in North Dakota in my twenties.

Outside those early family stories I heard as a child, the theater was my first real exposure to effective storytelling. To see stories come alive, with real, breathing characters, always amazed and delighted me. When "The Bishop Comes For a Visit" was first performed in 1996, I was struck for the first time by how a story in dramatic form can truly capture and affect people.

As I handed the manuscript of these 15 stories and one play around for critiques from various writer friends of mine, I was consistently amused to hear a common moniker: "Prairie Gothic." I reluctantly claim such a description, realizing that in doing so, there was no intent on my part to impart a common theme or "Gothic flavor" to the stories. They, like my poems, are often simply the end results of my various obsessions. Obsessions for any writer will, of course, find their way into the stories the writer tells. All I can do is acknowledge this obsession, accept it, live with it and, ultimately, use it.

Jamie Parsley
Fargo, North Dakota
June 2014

1

"AND THE MORNING STARS SANG..."

THE DOWNSTAIRS TENANT

∎

Downstairs.

No matter how hard he tried, that was all Melford Dunville kept thinking of that Sunday night.

Downstairs.

Downstairs.

Even as he knelt on the floor listening, his flabby side aching and the bones in his spine straining uncomfortably against one another, all he could think about was *downstairs*.

"What are you doing?" his wife asked. Caught by surprise, he jerked back from the metal grille with a start and glanced over his shoulder at her. She stood, fat and pink-faced, in the doorway between the kitchen and the living room, her hair rolled up in juice cans.

"I'm not doing nothing," he mumbled as he slowly and painfully struggled up from the living room floor with a wheezing groan. As he stood up, music began coming from Mrs. Rodriguez's apartment upstairs. After a moment, he recognized the song as "A Man and a Woman," played so loud the ceiling shuddered.

"Ashamed!" his wife tsked, ignoring the music. "That's what you should be. Ashamed."

"Why don't you just mind your own damned business?" he asked, shaking his head at her.

She rolled her eyes at him. "You should take a good, long, hard look at yourself, Melford. If you did, you'd be ashamed by what you saw."

"Oh, shaddup," he hissed as he moved toward his easy chair in front of the television.

"Ashamed," she continued. "I don't even want to show my face in public."

"I'm sure everyone's just gonna cry over *that*, Opal" Melford mumbled as he sank down into the chair and reached for a pack of a cigarettes and a lighter from the end table nearby. "Boo hoo hoo," he taunted. "What a travesty!"

"You wait," she said as she approached him, a chubby finger pointed at his face. "You just wait. That boy'll find out what you're doing. He'll find out and he'll call the Better Business Bureau on you. Or worse. The cops. And then what?"

"He's not gonna call the cops," Melford groaned, trying to peer around his wife at the television.

"Are you sure?" she continued. "Well, I'm always reading stories like that in the newspaper. Peeping Tom landlords, spying on their tenants. They don't go easy on the curious, you know."

"Jesus Christ!" he growled through clenched teeth. "Could you move? I'm trying to watch the friggin' TV."

She stood quietly where she was, her pink bathrobe hanging in billows beneath her stomach. After a few moments of pursing her lips worryingly at him, she turned with a creak of the floorboards and disappeared into the kitchen.

As the blue light of the television played over his face, he drug deeply on the cigarette he had just lit. The music upstairs ended. There was a pause. Then, the same song began again. Exhaling, Melford let his gaze wander slowly back across the room toward the vent in the floor.

"I'll tell you what, I know that kid's up to something," Melford finally blurted to his wife Tuesday evening as they lay side by side in bed. He had been watching the television between his toes while she read a romance magazine beside him. As soon as he said it, Melford regretted it. And yet, somehow, he knew he couldn't keep his suspicions inside any longer.

"Melford," Opal mumbled without looking up from her magazine. "He's just a boy. A nice college boy."

"Yah, that's what he wants everyone to think," Melford said. "And that's what makes me leery of him. No one's that nice. No one's that quiet. No one's that polite. Not at that age. No, he's up to something."

"What exactly do you think he's up to?" Opal asked, cocking her head toward him.

"I don't know," Melford said. "But I'm going to find out."

"You're getting paranoid, Melford," Opal said, turning her attention back to magazine. "That's not good. It's gonna get you in trouble. And then what are you gonna do?"

"Shaddup," Melford mumbled as he moved his feet a little farther apart so he could better see the television.

On Wednesday afternoon, Melford heard music in the grille.

"What is that?" he asked himself, trying to name the tune.

"What's what?" Opal called from the kitchen where she was making lunch.

"Oh, Jesus," he mumbled under his breath. "Nothing," he called back to his wife.

"Well then, stop listening at that stupid grille and get in here and eat your lunch."

"Eat your lunch, Melford," he mimicked under his breath. "Eat your lunch."

With a groan, Melford got up off the floor, humming the tune quietly to himself.

"'Tina Marie!'" Mrs. Rodriguez exclaimed.

"What?" Melford asked. He looked down from the stepladder he had climbed to change the hall light in front of Mrs. Rodriguez's apartment and stared at the small, thin woman in the aqua blue duster.

"What?" Mrs. Rodriguez repeated, cupping a hand over her ear.

"You just said Tina Marie!" Melford shouted.

"Oh," she said. "It was that song you were humming. It's 'Tina Marie.' I was trying to figure out what it was and just now I got it. 'Tina Marie.'"

"'Tina Marie,'" Melford repeated as he slowly descended the ladder with the burned-out bulb.

"That Perry Como, he was something else, I tell you."

"Perry Como," Melford repeated as he put the bulb in a plastic bag and folded up the stepladder.

"Oh, Perry Como!" Mrs. Rodriguez said. "I loved Perry Como! I think

I bought every record that man ever put out."

But Melford wasn't listening. After putting the bag with the light bulb in his toolbox, he quickly made his way back down the stairs with the stepladder under one arm. Behind him, Mrs. Rodriguez stood at the top of the stairs.

"Hey!" she called, but Melford was already at his door on the main floor of the building.

"Hey," Mrs. Rodriguez repeated. "What about the broken lock on my door?"

But Melford had already closed the door to his apartment behind him.

"You tell me what kind of kid listens to music like that in this day and age?" Melford asked as he sat beside his wife that night in the living room, watching television.

"How many times do I have to tell you," Opal said as she doubled-purled a square into the pink and gray afghan she was knitting. "You don't know it was Perry Como. Mrs. Rodriguez is deaf as a doornail. She sits up there playing that music all day and night. Loud as can be. I'm sure that tune has been running through her head for years."

"OK," the man shot back. "*You* listen and you tell me what it sounds like." And with that, he began humming the tune that had been playing over and over again in his head for the last day so loudly, spit wetting his lower lip. "So?" he finally asked when he was done.

"So what?" his wife groaned. "I couldn't tell what that was."

"Well then, listen again," Melford said.

"No," Opal said firmly. "I don't want to hear it again. I'm not going to be a party to *this*. You should see yourself, Melford. You're going insane. You're absolutely obsessed."

"So tell me," Melford persisted.

"Tell you what, Melford?" she asked impatiently.

"Does it sound like Perry Como to you?"

"I don't know," his wife said with an exhausted heave. She tossed down her knitting and slowly rocked her way up out of the chair. "And to be honest, I just don't care. But I'll tell you one thing, I'm not going to have a hand in any of this craziness. You want to get yourself all worked up over absolutely nothing, go ahead. I'm going to bed."

And with that, she made her way quietly to the bedroom, shutting the door firmly behind her.

Melford sat back in his chair and lit another cigarette. Watching the orange tip of the cigarette glow against the backdrop of the television screen, he quietly hummed his nameless tune to himself.

The kid came in late. When Melford heard the creak on the stairs going down to the basement apartment, he sat bolt upright in bed. He glanced over at the alarm clock on Opal's night stand.

"Two o'clock in the morning," he muttered. "See! See!" he gasped to his wife, whose wide back was turned to him, "There *is* something going on down there."

His wife responded with a grunting snore.

Melford carefully made his way out of bed and through the dark apartment to the vent. Getting down on his hands and knees, he leaned close to the grille and listened. After several moments, his face screwed up tightly with anguish.

"Nothing," he whispered, trying with every ounce of strength in him not to pound at the grille. "Nothing. Not a damned thing!"

Early that Friday afternoon, Opal went shopping and left Melford alone for the first time in a week to simply lie down on the floor beside the grille and listen to his heart's content. And throughout the afternoon, that is exactly what he did. His ear to the grille, he listened for any sound to come up through the vent to his living room. When he finally sat up, his back made a loud cracking sound and the pain in his spine brought tears to his eyes.

Finally, the pressure in Melford's head built to an agonizing crescendo. Leaning into the grille, he whispered, "Do something!" When he repeated it, it was no longer a whisper but a plea. "Do something." Finally he growled, "Do something! Do something! Do *some*thing!"

He crawled onto his hands and knees and, from that position, managed to stand up by using the nearby easy chair. His back cracked and shifted.

"Just do *something*!" he hissed as he stood up to his full height, panting heavily and feeling light-headed. He swayed over the grille and kicked at it with his patent-leather loafer.

"Come on, damn you! Do something!"

His body tensed as he pounded the grating with the back of his heel. His head swam dizzily as he felt the room beginning to spin.

"Do some …"

But he wasn't able to finish what he began. Swaying from the rush of blood flowing into his head, he felt himself fall backward. All the way down, he struggled to regain his balance. With a loud, rippling crack, his head connected with the corner of the heavy end table that separated his easy chair from his wife's.

When Opal came home from shopping that afternoon, she found a handwritten note taped to the door of her apartment.

Dear Mr. Dunville,
    Could you please keep the noise down upstairs. I have been trying very hard to study for finals. I need as much peace and quiet as possible at this time. I appreciate it.
                      Larry O'Connell
                      your downstairs tenant

Frowning as she stood in the hallway, reading the note, she fumbled with the doorknob and stepped into the apartment.

"Melford," she called out as she struggled with her shopping bags in one hand and the note in the other. "You're never going to believe the note we received from the down …"

But, as she stepped into the apartment and her eyes focused on the dimness inside, she realized she would be unable to ever finish the sentence.

ITA'S BABY

■

"Just go see him," Tom Bannon said to his wife as he leaned back in the kitchen chair. Only moments before, he had been eating his breakfast in silence, hidden away from his wife behind his morning newspaper. But now as he finished with his coffee and the paper had been read and re-read thoroughly, he turned his attention reluctantly back to his wife.

"I'm not going to see a minister," Ita Bannon said wearily. She was sitting across from him in her pink robe, reading her fourth magazine that morning. She had long ago lost count of how many cigarettes she had smoked since she got out of bed at four o'clock that morning, despite her promise to keep her habit in check.

Her husband was insistent. He folded the paper and moved his head in a circular motion, working his neck muscles. "Father Holmes knows about these things. He knows how to deal with these matters."

Please," she pleaded.

"It's time, though." He looked at her with a determined stare. "Don't you think it's time?" When she made no response, "It *is* time."

She merely shrugged and flipped the page of her magazine.

Tom looked at his wife with his mouth slightly open. She looked terrible, he thought. Her hair all done up in those ridiculous green plastic rollers and that dirty robe hanging, loose and billowing, from her skinny shoulders. Puffy gray bags hung beneath her bloodshot eyes. Her brand-new horn-rimmed glasses hung on the end of her nose as she read. Fighting a frown that tensed his face, he looked away from her and took another loud sip of coffee.

"How many hours of sleep did you get last night anyhow?" he asked as he stared into the bottom of his coffee cup.

She shrugged as she turned another page of the magazine.

"Did you sleep at all?"

She closed the magazine and tossed it aside as she stood up from her chair. "Finished?" she asked as she reached across the table for his empty plate.

"Yes, I am," he said, nodding. Then, "I know what you're going to say even before I say it …"

"Then why say it?" she asked, shrugging.

"… I think you should go see him."

"Christ," she mumbled as she turned on the sink faucet and let hot water run over his dirty dishes.

"That psychologist …" he started.

"… psychiatrist …" she corrected.

"… that psychiatrist isn't helping. You know that. You're no better now than you were a year ago."

"Nineteen months," she corrected again. When the sink began to fill with steam, she squeezed out a gob of liquid soap from a plastic bottle, watching as the water turned milky. Soapsuds formed and collected on the surface. The steam rose over her tired face, making her glasses fog and her eyes water. "I'm not going to see any minister," she said.

"Jesus, you are stubborn," he said, his voice hard and unrelenting. "You have to do something."

"What?" she asked without turning around. "*What* should I do?"

"You should …" He broke off when he knew she wasn't even going to turn from the sink to look at him.

"I told you once," she said, scrubbing his breakfast dish until it squeaked. "And I know I'll tell you again. I will never step foot in that church—or any other, for that matter—ever again in my life."

He groaned. "Don't be ridiculous."

"I'm not being ridiculous," she said calmly over the sound of the water pouring from the faucet. "I'm being honest."

He was quiet a moment, staring at her back. "You've got to believe in something. Who knows? Maybe that's all you need to pull you out of this …" He struggled for the word.

"This what?" she asked as she rinsed the dish.

"This *mess* you're in."

"Mess," she repeated, smiling slightly as the water washed the soapsuds from the dish's surface.

"A little faith might help," he said.

She was quiet as she set the plate in the strainer.

"Not believing doesn't help anything," he continued.

She was now scrubbing the smaller plate on which she served him his toast. Even after it was perfectly clean, she continued to scrub it. The squeaking sound almost drowned out his voice.

"It's not going to hurt anything," her husband went on. "It's not like he's going to convert you or anything."

She was still scrubbing at the small plate.

"He knows how to deal with situations like *this*," he said.

"Like what exactly?" she asked. She had stopped scrubbing and was now looking up from the sink out the window above the sink into the backyard. A pair of sparrows were being chased from the cement birdbath by a large yellow-eyed crow.

"He knows you're an …" His voice faltered.

"What?" she asked. "He's knows I am a what?"

"He knows you're an … atheist."

"I don't like that word," she said, watching the frightened sparrows take flight.

"Well, whatever you are …"

"… and how does he know *that*?" she asked, glancing over her shoulder at him.

A guilty look came up on his face. "I told him," he said simply.

She turned back to the window. The crow was eating the stolen seeds from the birdbath with a greedy furtiveness. Ita shifted her weight from one leg to the other and, as she did, the crow stopped eating and raised its head. For a moment, she thought it was looking right at her through the window with its cold side-long yellow eye.

"Just go and see the minister," Tom repeated from behind her.

She was quiet. She breathed in and out once and waited. The crow looked away and flew off suddenly.

"Ita."

"I believe in myself," she said and set the small plate into the strainer next to the larger one.

Unseen by his wife, Tom's face softened. "I don't think that's enough," he said.

She scrubbed at his fork now with a small steel sponge. "It has to be enough," she said quietly. She heard him shift in his chair.

"Look at everything your father got from his faith," Tom said.

Ita stiffened at the sink. She scrubbed the fork so hard with the steel sponge she could see little streaks forming on the stainless steel surface. "Yah," she said. "Look what it got him."

"Ita ... honey ..."

"I'm not going to that minister," she said firmly.

Her husband exhaled slowly. He picked up his coffee cup and sipped from it loudly. "I just wish you could see things my ..."

"You're going to be late," Ita interrupted, glancing over her shoulder at the plastic clock on the wall above the refrigerator.

"I'm going to be late," Tom repeated with desperation as he raised his wrist and looked at his watch. He stood up. Finally, she turned, the fork still in her wet hands. He grabbed his suit jacket from the back of his chair and slipped it onto his shoulders.

His kiss was still warm and wet, smelling a little of coffee, on her lips as she watched him from the open kitchen door. He lifted the garage door and slowly backed the Dodge out, braking once in front of the door to smile at her and wave a quick salute. She smiled faintly — she knew it would look sad to him — and blew him a kiss as he backed the car slowly down the driveway. She waited until the car disappeared down the street before she closed the door and turned back into the kitchen to clear his coffee cup and saucer from the table. She lit another cigarette and turned on the radio above the sink, filling the room with a gentle humming music. Bright yellow sunlight fell into the kitchen through the frail opaque curtain over the window above the sink. After the dishes were dried and placed back in the cupboards, all the silverware meticulously wiped and in the drawers and the dirty linens down the laundry chute, she went upstairs, where she bathed and dressed. She came downstairs and, fetching her purse and hat, she made her way to the still-open garage. Slowly she backed her Plymouth out onto the street. By ten thirty that morning, she was driving slowly down Third Avenue toward the cross juncture of Main Street.

On Main, she parked in front of the Kjelland Department Store. She stepped from the car, ground out another cigarette on the sidewalk and stepped toward the store. As she did, she caught a glimpse of her own reflection in the large display window. Her light-colored hair was done up neatly under her hat, her glasses were placed squarely atop the bridge of her nose. She padded a stray strand of hair into place beneath the hat before entering the store.

"Ita, dear!" Ophelia Kjelland heralded from behind the front counter as the bell above the door lightly announced Ita's entrance. The plump, pale-faced woman stood, fenced in on one side by the cash register, on the other by a large candy display.

"Hello, Mrs. Kjelland," Ita said as she made her way past the shopping cart carousel.

"Are *those* your new glasses, dear?"

"Do you like them?" Ita asked, lifting them a bit from her nose and waving them in Ophelia's direction.

"Do I like them? I love them! Oh, my! They're so much classier than these dowdy old things." Ophelia straightened her own wire-rimmed frames. "You know what I should do?"

"What should you do?" Ita asked playfully.

"I should go down there to Dr. Steiger's myself and seriously consider investing in a pair of plastic frames."

"You should," Ita called back as she made her way toward the back of the store. "You won't regret it."

In the rear of the store, there was a single aisle covered over with an arching floor-to-ceiling wooden trellis. Wired to the wooden plats were a large display of artificial flowers of every kind. Ita slowly walked beneath the wooden arch, first one way and then the other, her gloved hands reaching out for an occasional plastic rose or lilac. Finally, in one far corner of the trellis, her eyes fell upon a small white cluster of baby's breath. Carefully reaching above her head, she untied the wire stem and wrested it free from the wooden frame. Inspecting it carefully, testing the stiff plastic petals and leaves, she nodded to herself and turned on her heel, back down the aisle toward the counter.

"It is the twenty-third already?" Mrs. Kjelland asked as searched the bouquet for the price tag. She paused to glance at a small calendar attached to the side of the cash register.

"You know my schedule better than I do," Ita said.

"Well, you know something, I think tradition is a dying art. I really do. Most people these days seem like they could care less for it. So, it's refreshing when someone your age does what you do." She leaned across the counter for a paper bag. "Ten cents, dear."

Ita handed the dime across the counter.

"Yes," Mrs. Kjelland continued as she dropped the dime into the cash drawer. "You certainly don't see many people your age keeping tradition. Much less going out to the cemetery to tend graves."

Ita forced a smile that hurt her face.

"But not you, dear," Ophelia went on, putting the receipt in the little paper bag with the bouquet. "No, not you. I swear, your baby must have the best-kept grave in Pinkham Heights Cemetery."

Ita's smile lengthened. She rubbed her forefinger and thumb together craving a cigarette.

"How long has it been?" Ophelia asked.

Ita's smile tightened into a grim pursing of her lips. "Nineteen months." The words hung hard and sour just beyond her lips.

Ophelia shook her head, clicking her tongue as she did. "You poor, poor thing. First your father. Then, right after, your baby." She clicked her tongue again, louder. Then, smiling, she said, "You know, I'd think I'd see you more often in church."

Ita stiffened, taking the bag from Ophelia.

"That handsome young husband of yours is always there," Ophelia said. "Alone. But never you."

"Thank you, Mrs. Kjelland," Ita said as she turned from the counter and made her way for the door.

"Say a prayer for me while you're at the cemetery, dear!" Ophelia called as Ita clumsily made her way through the front door.

Say a prayer for me.

The words thudded in Ita's head as she slowly maneuvered the Plymouth from the curb in front of the department store and out onto Main Street.

Say a prayer for me.

"Is it really so hard, Ita Jean?" her father asked her as the older man laid back on the stiff hospital pillow. "Can't you say even one little prayer for me?"

"How?" Ita asked. "How can I?"

"Ita Jean," her father pleaded through the oxygen tent that surrounded his bed.

Ita shook her head and slipped a hand through a slit in the plastic draping, grasping her father's hand tightly. She was always amazed at how big his hands were. Even now. The skin was waxy and tight. She could feel thick, purple veins against her palm. Ita squeezed tighter and felt the bones in her father's hands shift against each other. His fingers squeezed back weakly. Ita leaned close to the plastic and her father's blurred face. The strong line of his jaw swam in her eyes.

"Squinting again," he chided. A faint smile quivered on his lips. "You've got to get those eyes checked before the baby comes." He nodded at Ita's swollen stomach.

"I know," Ita said, nodding. "I will."

"And you pray," he commanded.

Ita shook her head.

"Don't you believe any more?"

Ita sighed, shaking her head.

"Why?" her father asked.

Ita shrugged.

"That's not an answer."

Ita breathed deeply.

"I just don't," Ita said. She touched the oxygen tank with her free hand. "I can't explain it."

"Try to explain it," her father said, squeezing his fingers around his daughter's.

"Well, for one thing, look at this." She motioned at the tent with her head. "Look at what's happened to you. Where is …" Her voice trailed off.

"Ita," her father said. "It doesn't work like that."

"If it doesn't work like that, then what's the use?" Ita asked. Her voice was quivering in her throat.

"Oh, Ita Jean," her father mourned. "Just try. Please. For me."

Ita nodded. Her father closed his eyes and started to move his lips quietly. Ita hesitantly bowed her head and looked down at her brown shoes. No words came into her head. All she heard was the low whirring of the oxygen coming from a tall canister in the corner of the room. Ita swallowed hard and looked more intently at her shoes. One of the straps was worn down at the crease. She let her gaze move to her stomach, round and hard, beneath her maternity blouse. Her father squeezed her hand and Ita looked up at her father's face.

"So?" her father asked with a hopeful look on his face.

Ita forced a smile. Her father's excited look faded.

"My poor dear," her father whispered. "My poor, poor dear." Then, after a moment. "Pray, Ita Jean. Just pray."

Pray. Pray. Pray.

As Ita drove south down Main Street and out of town, past the new addition of prefabricated houses and the large billboard near the street proclaiming SOUTH WIND ESTATES: YOUR FUTURE IS *NOW*, she turned the radio's volume up. Nat King Cole was singing "A Blossom Fell." With the music playing, she stopped at a stop sign a quarter of a mile south of town and turned east on the highway.

A blossom fell
From off a tree
It settled softly on the lips you turned to me.

As she drove, she glanced at the paper bag on the seat beside her. The wire stem, thinly encased in almost opaque light green plastic, poked out from a tear in the bottom of the bag. She breathed deeply, then begin to sing along with the song on the radio.

"I thought you loved me
You said you loved me
We planned together
To dream forever
The dream has ended
For true love died
The night a blossom fell
And touched two lips that lied."

The highway before her undulated smoothly through the rolling hills outside town. The morning sun fell, dull and colorless, on the gray pavement. In front of her car, a large grain truck with a bright red rack moved slowly, hugging the pale middle divider line. Watching the truck's vibrating tail, its license plate swinging loose from one screw, she felt a headache gnawing through her forehead. She adjusted the glasses atop her nose.

A blossom fell
And very soon
I saw you kissing someone new beneath the moon ...

Ita turned off the highway onto a narrow gravel road which circled around a steep hill. At the crest of the hill was a tree-covered peak, surrounded by a rusting metal fence. She maneuvered the car through a black iron archway with PINKHAM HEIGHTS CEMETERY in bold Germanic lettering and followed the road to the right as it wound along the outer edge of the cemetery.

As she drove beneath the trees, she glanced at the stones on both sides of the road. The engraved names showed clearly in the morning light that fell through the trees overhead. Since all of the names were so familiar to her, she tried to find one that she didn't recognize.

"Puiyer," she recited to herself. "Tinquist. Donnely. Fughere."

Near the front of the cemetery, where the monuments were oldest, she spied a white, moss-covered gravestone. She read the inscription aloud, "Ahnonnen Family." The first judge of Simpson County, she remembered her father saying when was a young girl every time they came here to visit her mother's grave.

"Hibbert," Ita read from a much newer, though no less-impressive stone. She remembered this one very clearly. Beneath the headstone lay seven family members—mother, father, four children and grandmother—all killed only two miles from this spot in a fiery car-train collision in the early autumn of 1950 that garnered national news reports.

"Krober," she read the engraved letters on a tall, cobalt-colored marble pillar near the Hibbert stone, which marked the graves of the former president of the Farmer's Union Bank and his wife. Ita had graduated from high school with their granddaughter.

And just up the hill from it, a stone with a name she did not read aloud. HEIDT, in pale lettering. Her own maiden name. The stone was simple, a plain gray square of marble, unremarkable compared with the grander monuments that surrounded it. From the road she could read the small subsquares beneath the banner surname. KATHERINE J. 1900-1943, her mother, dead now all these twelve years from tuberculosis. And beside it, FRANCIS K. 1898-1954.

Ita touched the brake lightly until the Plymouth rolled quietly to a stop. She sat behind the steering wheel, silently contemplating the stone. From the road, she could see the still-raw dirt of her father's grave in the grass. In the shadows the trees overhead cast down on the gravesite, Ita was overcome with sadness at how plain and bare the graves looked without flowers.

The trees whispered as breeze blew through them. Ita breathed in and out. Her gaze slowly moved away from her parents' gravestone and settled on the stone of a name she did not know. HIATT. She frowned at the name and tried to picture faces to go with the name, but none came into her head. She stared at the stone for several moments, reading and re-reading the epitaph at the bottom of the stone: IN YOUR KINDNESS, REMEMBER US, WE PRAY.

Pray, Ita's mind reeled. *Pray. Pray.*

"The Lord be with you," the Reverend Samuel Edward Holmes, rector of St. Bartholomew-by-the-Lake Episcopal Church, intoned into the cold February air as he stood at the foot of the casket that contained the body of Frank Heidt. The sharp winter wind caused a ripple to move through the minister's white surplice.

"And with thy spirit," the mourners gathered around the grave responded in unison, except for Ita, who sat in a metal folding chair beside the casket. Tom stood behind her, his gloved hands on her shoulders.

"In sure and certain hope of the Resurrection to eternal life through our Lord Jesus Christ," the minister said, "we commit the body of this child to the ground. The Lord bless him and keep, the Lord make his face to shine upon him and be gracious unto him, the Lord lift up his countenance upon him and give him peace, both now and evermore."

"Amen," the mourners solemnly sang.

The bare trees overhead creaked in the strong winter wind. Beyond the trees, the sky was heavy and gray. A small branch snapped loose and fell onto the metal lid of the casket. Ita watched the branch lie there until the funeral director, a short, plump man with a thick, black pompadour, stepped forward and brushed it off.

"May almighty God, the Father, the Son and the Holy Ghost, bless you and keep you, now and for evermore," the minister intoned.

"Amen," the mourners replied.

And with that, it was over. Father Holmes closed his red-covered *Book of Common Prayer* and turned from the grave. Ita could hear the crunching of feet behind her in the crisp snow as people turned and headed down the steep slope toward their still-running cars. Ophelia Kjelland, red-faced and shivering, stepped forward and offered Ita her condolences.

"I am so sorry, dear," Ophelia said, taking Ita's gloved hand in her own. "I don't know what to say to you right now."

Ita nodded, blank-faced, and squeezed Ophelia's hand. Mrs. Kjelland then turned away.

Tom squeezed Ita's shoulder.

"Let's go," he whispered into her ear. His breath was hot and wet against her cold cheek. As he leaned forward, he noticed the thin trickle of sweat that made its way down her cheek from beneath her hat.

"Honey?" he asked.

She looked up at him as she rose, with an effort, from the folding chair.

"Are you all right?" Tom asked.

Ita nodded. As she stood beside her father's casket in the cold air, she swallowed deeply and turned away. She walked carefully — one foot in front of the other — atop the artificial grass laid out all around the open grave. Tom was at her side, one hand on the small of her back, the other holding her elbow, when the pain — dull and hot within her — shot through her body. She stumbled, the strength in her legs suddenly gone. She slipped from Tom's loose grasp and went down on her knees first. And then, slowly, she rolled onto her side in the snow piled just beyond the square of fake green grass.

"Oh ..." she groaned, her breath smoky and white in the cold air. Lying on the ground, on her side, with cold, grainy snow on the back of her neck, she felt herself losing consciousness quickly. She fought it despite the excruciating pain in her body. As her eyes rolled back into her sockets, she saw the naked tree branches overhead creaking against the stone gray sky. The last thing she heard was the voice of Mrs. Kjelland over the sound of crunching snow,

"The baby! Be careful of the baby! Oh, God!"

God.

Ita shivered. She shook her head, trying to jar the image of her father's casket loose. She glanced once more at her parents' gravestone before she let her foot off the brake and coasted down the road in low gear. At the rear of the cemetery, near the bottom of the slope, was a stretch of lawn between the road and the fence. In the grass lay row upon row of flush-lying stones. A hinged sign beside the road read BABYLAND.

Ita parked the car on the road and slipped off her gloves. She took the bouquet of flowers from the paper bag on the seat beside her and, getting out of the car, she adjusted her glasses and smoothed the crease in her skirt.

The grave was the fourth to the last in the last row of graves. Three graves finished out the row, marked with simple metal markers provided by the funeral home, placed in the still-fresh earth. The grave nearest her son was now almost a year old, the last grave was no more than a week old—a pitifully small mound of dirt only a few inches longer than Ita's foot. A spray of wilted blue carnations lay atop the fresh, black earth.

The stone marking Ita's baby's grave was new, set into the grass only the month before.

WILLIAM ANDREW BANNON
OUR DARLING BABY
FEBRUARY 24, 1954

Ita knelt in the cold, wet grass to the side of the stone. The late-morning sun had not yet gathered enough strength to burn off the thin layer of morning dew. She leaned across the grave and wiped a wet leaf from the engraved name. She then inserted the wire stem of the fake baby's breath into the dirt around the gravestone. When she was done, she sat back and took in the grave at her knees. The faint outline of the grave still showed through the thin layer of grass that had grown over the grave. She searched the new green grass until her eyes grew tired and sore.

She sighed deeply and looked away. The cemetery's hill flowed downward beyond the fence line toward a wheat field, where it leveled off. She followed the field until it disappeared over another hill about a mile away. A breeze came out of the south and caressed the golden wheat. She slowly let her gaze move upward into the trees overhead. A branches full of leaves moved slightly in the wind, rocking back and forth against the sky. She heard a crow caw twice somewhere above her. Then she let her gaze drift back to the gravestone.

"William," she whispered, reading the chiseled name aloud. "Bill." She shook her head. "Billy." She grimaced, then read the next name on the stone aloud. "Andrew." She nodded. "Andy." The word was heavy and sour in the back of her mouth. "William Andrew."

A black ant crawled over the flat stone, slowly making its way toward her bent knee. She watched it until it covered the distance of the stone and disappeared into the grass. She looked back at the grave.

"Bones," she said aloud. "Just bones."

Bones

"That's all that's left," the short, fat pompadoured funeral director responded to her question as he sat behind his desk in the office of the Durer-Zeitung Funeral Home. "Bone fragments. Some ashes. It isn't fine, like you think. It's not like cigarette ash. It's more like ..." He struggled to find the right image. "It's almost like oatmeal."

Ita frowned.

"Ita," Tom reasoned. "We're not going to have the baby cremated."

"I know," Ita said. "I was just ..."

"No," Tom said emphatically, cutting her off in mid-sentence.

"I was just asking a question," Ita said, finishing her sentence.

"Besides, it's not a smart idea," Al Durer, the funeral director, said. "It's a very long, drawn-out process. We have no crematoriums in North Dakota."

"Really?" Tom said, nodding.

"No," Al said. "The nearest one is in the Twin Cities. So, we have to ship the remains by train to Minneapolis for cremation. And then, the cremains are shipped back. It takes several days."

Ita nodded as she sat in the overstuffed chair.

"Why did you even bring it up?" Tom asked. He looked at her from the chair next to hers, his face crumpled with disappointment.

"You know why," Ita said.

"No, I don't."

Ita looked at the funeral director with an embarrassed smile.

"Let's just talk about it later," Ita said without barely moving her lips.

"No," Tom said. "I want know why you're so set on this."

"Because," Ita began and then let her voice trail off.

"Why?" Tom asked persistently.

"Because, Tom," she said quietly. "I'm tired.

"We're all tired," Tom said. "We're all drained by this."

"I'm tired of graves, Tom. No more graves."

"Oh, God," Tom exclaimed, looking away from her toward the window.

"No more funerals," Ita continued.

"Well, we need to have a funeral," Tom said.

"Oh, yes," Al Durer piped in. "There *must* be some sort of ceremony."

"Yes, there will be a funeral," Tom said.

"For the living," Al said. "If for no one else, for the living."

"I'm tired of gravestones and flowers and ..." Her voice trailed off once again.

Tom and Ita looked away from each other, Tom out the window of the office, Ita at the legs of the desk in front of her. She was tired and sore and her mind was reeling with a fuzzy numbness.

"I don't even know why you're suggesting this," Tom said without looking at her.

"Because I'm tired," Ita said.

"Yah, you said that already," Tom said. "We both are."

Ita looked back at the funeral director, who met her gaze with a pursed, embarrassed smile. She tried to plead with him with her eyes, but when he looked down at the papers in front of him nervously, she knew that he would be no help.

Ita slumped deeper into the overstuffed chair. "All right," she said.

"You'll forget about cremation?" Tom asked.

"Yes," she said, looking down at the legs of the desk again.

"And there will be a funeral?" Al Durer said, looking back and forth between Tom and Ita.

"Yes," Ita said wearily.

"Very good," the funeral director said, rubbing his hands together. "Next, we need to pick out a casket."

Ita suddenly felt nauseous.

"We have several beautiful models in the showroom," Al Durer said, rising from his chair with a wheeze. "Will you follow me?"

Tom stood up from his chair and touched Ita's shoulder. Without looking at either of the men, she stood on shaking legs. As they followed the funeral director down a long, dark hallway, Tom whispered into Ita's ear, "Thank you."

"For what?" Ita asked.

"For doing *this*," he said, waving ahead of him at the funeral director's back.

The funeral director opened a door and stepped into a large room, turning on the light. As Ita and Tom stepped in, she looked about her at the room filled with caskets. She stiffened. This was the second time she had been in this room in a month. Nearest the door was the same blue metal casket model she had picked for her father. Now Al Durer led them toward the back of the room, where there were three small coffins laid out side by side. The first was covered in pink velvet.

"This is our least expensive model," Durer said, lifting the lid. "It has a simple satin lining with a pillow." He pressed on the pillow to show how much stuffing it had. "It also comes, of course, in blue and a plain white."

Tom looked at his wife. "So?"

Ita shrugged wearily.

"It looks like a shoebox," Tom said to the funeral director. "What about this one?" He was motioning toward a slightly larger casket made of mahogany.

"Oh, this is one of our finest," the funeral director said, opening the upper half of the lid. The hinges whispered and the naked light overhead glinted off the polished surface. "This also has a satin lining, but it also has padding. And the pillow is more durable. Plus, this is guaranteed." He pointed to a small cardboard card attached to the foot of the coffin.

"Guaranteed?" Ita asked. "Guaranteed for what?"

"To stay together," the funeral director said. "For fifty years."

Tom looked at Ita with a slight smile and then turned back to the casket. He ran his fingers over the polished wood surface and then, inside, the satin lining.

"Fifty years, you say?" Tom said.

"Yes," Al Durer said, nodding. "It's peace of mind."

"Peace of mind," Tom said looking back at his wife, nodding. "Peace of mind guaranteed for fifty years."

For fifty years.
"Fifty years," Ita said aloud as she shifted her weight from one folded leg to the other beneath her. She grunted with disgust and searched the surface of the stone for something, although she didn't know what exactly she was looking for. She reached out and touched the cold, dew-wet surface of the stone with her bare hand.

Just bones, she thought.

Her voice broke off. She slipped off her glasses and neatly folded the bows. With her free hand, she covered her eyes. Her breath quivered as the pain rose up inside her but she didn't—she couldn't—cry. Her eyes stung with dryness.

Her breath heaved again and slowly she exhaled. It was a long breath Ita Bannon let out—complete and cleansing. Her body slowly relaxed, beginning with her shoulders and working downward. She shifted her weight back onto the heels of her shoes folded beneath her.

Looking away from the grave, she gazed up again. The sky beyond the canopy of trees was blue and cloudless above her.

And there, nothing, either, she thought. *Nothing but sky.*

The crow cawed once more and the sound of it, for some reason, soothed her.

She rose from the grave after another several moments. It was a quick, fluid movement. Her knees cracked, her back shifted into place. She stood over her son's grave, her knees cold with the wet dew trapped between her nylons and her skin. The shadows of the branches overhead moved on the stone as the breeze whispered again. And for the first time in a very long time, she smiled. It was barely a movement in the tensed muscles of her face, but even it surprised her. She let the smile move on her lips until she no longer felt like smiling. Then she turned and walked toward the car.

The crow cawed yet again in the trees above her.

In the Plymouth, she put her glasses back on. The gauzy world of a moment before was suddenly made clear for her. She adjusted the glasses atop her nose as she looked at her reflection in the rearview mirror. Then, she turned on the ignition and shifted into gear. As she slowly made her way through the cemetery, she heard the last strains of "April in Portugal" on the radio, followed by the weatherman solemnly intoning the day's weather report,

"KGTI Weather forecast today calls for scattered showers this afternoon and into the evening with a possible thunderstorm during the night."

Then, Ray Anthony began playing "Skokiaan."

She looked up through the windshield as she drove toward the cemetery gate. Above the black trees, there was only empty blue sky.

"Not even a cloud in the sky," she said to herself.

And with that, she maneuvered the car down the gravel road toward the highway.

THE DOWNSTAIRS TENANT by Jamie Parsley

LEELAND FRANKEN'S BIBLE

■

Raymond Halvorson was reading a paperback titled *Bloody Murder is Passion Red* on the front porch when his father's black pickup turned off the highway and onto the dirt road that led to the farm. A thick cloud of dust rose behind the truck as it bumped loudly along, circled the driveway once and then shuddered to a stop in front of a restored chicken coop, painted white to match the house. Raymond's father got out first and walked to the small building. And then the passenger—an old man—withdrew stiffly from the cab of the pickup. He straightened his back, looked about the farm yard, his gaze pausing on the coop, and then reached back into the truck to bring out a stained, taped-together cardboard suitcase. The old man followed Raymond's father into the small building.

Raymond's mother stepped out onto the porch.

"You think he would've learned after the last one," she mumbled. "Where does he find them, anyway?"

"They hang around the Co-op in town," Raymond reminded her, not looking up from his book.

His mother walked to the edge of the porch and stood there, her hands on her hips. Her apron blew up at her face as a sudden gust of warm wind blew in from the south. She quickly smoothed the apron back against her legs with a frustrated grunt.

"He looks like a lush, doesn't he?" she asked, peering over the edges of her wire-rimmed glasses just as her husband and the old man emerged from the coop.

"I don't know," Raymond shrugged, looking up from his book. "He looks clean to me."

His mother nodded.

"Better than that last one."

Raymond rolled his eyes in anticipation of what she was going to say next.

"You know, it took me a week and a half to clean up that hole after he left. A week and a half!"

"I know," Raymond mumbled. "A week and a half."

"I had to rip up the damned linoleum!"

"You had to rip it up," Raymond repeated as he gazed at his book.

"I carried out three garbage cans full of beer bottles."

"Yup. Three garbage cans," Raymond intoned.

"*That's* what that bastard did!" his mother huffed.

Raymond didn't say anything more. He just looked at the words on the pages of the book.

Raymond's father spotted his wife and son on the porch and waved his hand at them. He then led the old man toward the house.

"Oh, wonderful!" Raymond's mother moaned under her breath as they approached. "Here they come."

Raymond didn't look up from his book.

"This is my wife, Esther," Raymond's father said to the old man. "And this is my son, Raymond. *This* is LeeLand Franken. He's gonna help out around here, hopefully until harvest?" He looked at the old man with a questioning look.

"Hopefully," the old man replied.

"Mr. Franken," Esther Halvorson mumbled. She tilted her head back, thrusting out her jaw at him. Otherwise, she made no movement of greeting. The old man raised his dusty hat at her.

"Raymond! Say hello!" his father demanded.

"Hello," Raymond mumbled, peering over the edge of the book.

The old man nodded at Raymond.

As his father and the old man turned and walked back to the coop, Raymond's mother hissed under her breath, "He had just better keep that place clean, or else he won't make it to harvest."

"'Scuse me," LeeLand Franken muttered with a nod after he had finished his supper and, slipping from his chair, knelt on the floor. Placing his elbows on the seat of his chair, he buried his face in his hands and mumbled quietly to himself. Then, with a groan, he rose stiffly from the floor and headed to the door, putting his hat atop his head.

Raymond's jaw dropped.

"What the hell was that?" he asked.

"That was rudeness personified!" his mother exclaimed. She had dropped her fork half-way into the display and still had not picked it up. She turned to her husband. "Have you ever?"

His father, who observed the man's praying with the same initial shock as his wife and son, smiled, chuckling to himself, and then resumed eating.

"Ah, there's nothing wrong with that," he said.

"Nothing wrong with that?" Esther hissed. "Are you serious?"

"It shows he's a good Christian man," her husband shrugged.

"Christian or not, that's just downright rude! Praying like — like *that*!" She waved her hand at the empty chair the old man had been sitting in. "And did you see him eat? His elbows on the table like that? I've never!" Esther threw her napkin into her plate, which was a declaration that she was finished eating.

Raymond simply sat back in his chair, shaking his head.

After supper, Raymond slowly walked past the coop on his way to the barn to look at the horses. The door to the coop was open slightly and a pale orange sliver of light edged the door frame. A voice came from within the coop.

"But thou, O Lord, knowest me; thou hast seen me, and tried mine heart toward thee: pull them out like sheep for the slaughter, prepare them for the day of slaughter."

Raymond paused, listening until the voice died away. He turned and was moving slowly toward the barn when he heard the old man.

"Know the passage?"

Raymond turned. The old man was holding the door of the coop wide open.

"No," Raymond said.

"Come here, then," the old man commanded.

Raymond made a step or two toward the coop.

"You're not at all familiar with Jeremiah?" the old man asked.

"No. Not at all."

The old man frowned at this answer.

"Don't you go to church?"

"No," Raymond said, shaking his head.

"Why?" the old man asked.

"I don't believe in church," Raymond said simply.

The old man frowned. "Yet, you seemed to be paying attention just now, when I was reading."

Raymond shrugged. "I like the way you read, that's all. I like your voice. You sound like one of those preachers on the radio."

The old man nodded. His dark eyes fell over the boy. "How old are you?"

"Nineteen."

The old man clicked his tongue. "What a shame," he said, shaking his head.

"What is?"

"Nineteen years old and crippled." The old man nodded at Raymond's aluminum crutches. "So, what happened?"

Raymond shifted his weight from one leg to the other. "It was a car accident."

The old man shrugged his skinny shoulders. His eyebrows arched and as they did, his forehead wrinkled. "Live by the sword, you die by it. I guess the same can be said of speed."

Raymond gasped. "That's not what happened at all."

The old man shrugged again. "It doesn't matter. It's too bad all the same." He looked the boy over once again. "So, is that why you're angry?"

"Angry? I'm not angry."

"Sure you are," the old man said. "You're angry at the Lord."

Raymond felt like laughing. "I'm not angry at anyone."

The old man smiled at this and stroked his thick, white mustache. "I know what I know—that's all I know—and I know you're not happy with your Maker."

Raymond struggled for the words to counter this, but, not finding them, he asked, "What makes you think that?"

The old man raised a gray gnarled finger to his temple "I have my ways."

"Your ways!" Raymond snorted, suddenly feeling an anger come up in him.

"The spirit moves ... and everything falls into place," the old man said.

Raymond felt his jaw stiffen. The old man read the hard look on the boy's face.

"Well, you know, if you're ever interested in knowing more about the Word, stop by anytime."

And with that, LeeLand Franken dismissed the boy by turning his back to him. He stepped back into his quarters, shutting the door tightly behind him without another word.

Raymond stood where he was, leaning on his crutches. For several moments, he stared at the closed door, pink now in the dying sunlight. A frown played on his face. Finally, with a grunt, he turned away and walked slowly toward the barn and the neighing horses.

The next day, while the old man and Raymond's father were out in the fields, Raymond stepped quietly up to the door of the converted chicken coop. Cautiously he opened it, looked around at the yard behind him, then stepped in. He could smell a dankness—a faint smell of stale liquor still lingering in the floor boards. But the white paint on the walls was fresh and the newly laid linoleum on the floor had a rubbery smell to it.

The cot with its coarse olive-colored army blanket was neatly made. Raymond could see one corner of the suitcase under the cot. He opened the top drawer of the old, battered dresser. Inside, the old man's few clothes — mostly plaid shirts and khaki trousers—were neatly folded and placed, side by side, in the drawers. Atop the dresser was the Bible the old man had been reading the night before. Raymond touched it carefully. The leather was worn smooth as skin and, in the unlit building, it took on a dark color. Its cracked cover bent slightly at a jagged crease, and the spine was worn gray by fingering. Propping his crutches beneath his arms, he picked up the book and flipped through it, seeing where the pages' red edges were smeared pink in places. Ink scorings throughout the book underlined particular passages.

Just as he was about to close it and set it back on the dresser, the book fell open to a series of pages between the Old and New Testaments made from a heavier-quality paper than the rest of the book. The first page, labeled OUR FAMILY HISTORY, had a marriage certificate. THIS CERITIFES THAT (in ink) *LeeLand Franken* AND (also in ink) *Thelma Nord-*

strom WERE UNITED IN HOLY MATRIMONY ON THE *15th* DAY OF *March* IN THE YEAR OF OUR LORD *1908*. The next page was entitled HUSBAND'S GENEALOGY, giving the birthdate of LeeLand Alexander Franken as July 25, 1887, at Isabella, Minnesota. Under WIFE'S GENEALOGY, Thelma Naomi Nordstrom Franken was born May 1, 1890, in Kindred, North Dakota, She died July 11, 1925, in Fargo, North Dakota, where she was buried. The OUR CHILDREN page had only one handwritten entry: Richard Jerome Franken, Born July 16, 1909, in Buhl, Minnesota. He died November 22, 1918, in Nevis, Minnesota.

Raymond held the book to his nose and inhaled deeply. The smell that filled his nostrils was heavy and musty—a warm, strangely comforting smell. He stood where he was for several moments, smelling the Bible until, suddenly, he caught a glimpse of his reflection in the cracked mirror above the dresser. There, disjointed in the broken glass, propped up on his crutches, he stared back at his own drawn, colorless face. He felt the blood run cold in his veins. He was amazed how sickly he looked in the half-light inside the building. His red hair looked dull and brittle and the freckles on his face were dark and splotchy. Raymond looked quickly away from his reflection and set the Bible back into its place atop the dresser.

As he exited the coop, he almost tripped on a corner of linoleum near the door that had curled upward from dampness. Only when he made it to the porch of the house did he stop, breathing heavily. A cold trickle of sweat ran down the side of his face, down his neck and into the collar of his shirt.

Raymond observed the old man closely that night at supper, memorizing every movement—the bowed head, the moving lips as he prayed quietly before supper, the slow, deliberate eating of his food, the way he excused himself politely and knelt at the chair praying before going back out to the coop.

"Crazy coot!" Raymond's mother hissed as she cleared the old man's empty plate from the table.

"He's sure a hard worker, though," Raymond's father said, his mouth full of mashed potatoes.

"He's certainly something different than I've ever seen," Raymond said.

"Sure, take *his* side," his mother replied from the sink. Turning her attention back to her husband, she said, "I suppose he prays before work?"

"As a matter of fact ..." Raymond's father mumbled.

Raymond walked out to the barn after supper again. As he passed the small building, he noticed it was quiet. The old man was not reading his Bible out loud. No sound at all came from behind the closed door. There was only the faint, orange light framing the door crack. On the way back to the house after visiting the horses, Raymond paused once more before the coop. Still, no sound. It was dark inside.

Raymond usually woke late in the morning, long after his father was well out in the fields. And so, next morning, Raymond was surprised to find his father sitting at the kitchen table slowly sipping his coffee, as he entered for breakfast. Raymond's mother sat across from her husband, her arms folded stiffly across her chest.

"What happened?" Raymond asked immediately when he read the hard looks in his parents' faces.

"The old man died last night," his father intoned.

Raymond was quiet as he stood in the doorway to the kitchen. His mother rose from the table and went to the oven, where she prepared a plate of hash browns and bacon for him.

"He died in his sleep, I guess," his mother said as she scraped the skillet.

Raymond went to the table and sat down. As his mother placed the plate before him, he felt what little appetite he awoke with leave him completely.

"Where is he now?" Raymond asked. "Is he still out there?"

"No," his father said, breathing on his hot coffee. "The hearse from the funeral home already took him away."

Absently, Raymond tapped at the food on his plate with his fork. He looked up at his parents. "What about his things?"

"I don't know," his father said, shaking his head. "I don't think he had any family."

Raymond looked down at the plate in front of him.

"I don't even know what they're going to do with him now. I don't know where he'll be buried. Or if there's anyone to pay for it."

"Well, *we're* not!" Raymond's mother snorted as she slumped into her chair across from her husband.

Raymond set his fork down and watched his food cool on the plate.

Raymond was sitting at the kitchen table that afternoon when his mother brought in the old man's cardboard suitcase from the coop and set it inside the back door, placing the Bible on top of it.

"The sheriff's coming out later this afternoon to get all this," Raymond's mother said to him as she entered the kitchen. "He'll know what to do with it." She nodded. "It's not our problem anymore."

Raymond watched her from the kitchen table with a steady stare as she moved across the room.

"What's your problem?" she asked when she saw the look on his face.

"So, how was the coop?" he asked.

"The coop?"

"Pretty messy, huh?" he asked.

His mother stopped near the oven and looked at him with a firmly set expression. He met it and held it until she finally looked away. Finally, she mumbled, "It was clean."

"Any beer?" Raymond asked.

She was biting her lip as she looked at the floor. "No," she managed. "Not a thing."

"So what *was* there?" he asked.

"Just some clothes," she said in low voice. "Some toiletries. The suitcase." She nodded toward the back entryway. "And, of course, a Bible." When she looked up at her son, he was nodding.

"Maybe," he said, "you were wrong about him after all."

She shot him a cold glance. "I'm going to make the beds," she said without looking at him and quickly left the kitchen.

He listened for her footsteps on the stairs going up to the second floor. When he heard her overhead, in her bedroom, he reached for his crutches under the table and stood up. He walked slowly to the suitcase in the rear entryway and brought the Bible back to the kitchen table, along with a ballpoint pen. He opened the book to the OUR FAMILY HISTORY pages and, under HUSBAND'S GENEALOGY, wrote June 5, 1961, in the entry marked DATE OF DEATH. Looking at the date, he sat back in his chair, the Bible's strong, heavy smell rose from the table and filled the room. Absently, he leafed through the book. One of the loose pages broke free and fell to the floor. As he picked it up, he saw that a passage on the page was circled. He read it once to himself, and then again, as the bright afternoon sunlight fell through the window onto the kitchen table in front of him.

His mother came down the stairs and was about to go to Raymond's bedroom, which was on the main floor, to make his bed when she heard him. She quickly made her way to the kitchen. "Raymond?" she called as she approached the doorway. "Is that you?"

"... and they were judged every man according to their words ..." he intoned as he sat hunched over the book.

"I almost didn't recognize your voice," his mother said as she entered the kitchen. "It didn't sound like you at all ..."

"... and death and hell were cast down into the lake of fire ..." He held the loose page from the book up in front of his face without looking at her.

"Raymond!" she called out. She crossed the kitchen and stood just beside him. "What are you doing?" She reached out, trying to grab the page from his hand, but he jerked away from her and kept on reading, his voice overtaking hers.

"... and whosoever was not found written in the book of life was cast into the lake of fire ..."

Only then did Raymond stop reading. He looked up at his mother, nodding and smiling slightly.

"Amen," Raymond intoned defiantly as he stared his mother down. "And amen!"

Then, his elbows on the table, he bowed his head and buried his face in hands, his lips moving slightly.

"Are you praying?" his mother asked as she stood over him. But even as she asked the question, she felt herself smile, because she, of course, knew better.

THE DOWNSTAIRS TENANT by Jamie Parsley

THE LETTER

■

Terry Schwer's last letter arrived Tuesday afternoon, the day his ashes came back from the crematory. His father, Ron Schwer, brought in the foot-tall brown tin canister from the car and set it on the mantelpiece above the fireplace in the den. He then carefully arranged two framed photos on each side of the box. One was Terry's graduation photo, his smooth cheeks dimpled by a wide grin, his dark hair combed neatly into place, a carefully knotted bow tie at his throat. The other photo showed Terry in a hockey uniform, his legs splayed slightly, knees bent inward toward each other, leaning over a hockey stick, his sweaty hair hanging in long strands in his eyes. He was smiling the same tooth-filled grin as in the companion photo.

Terry's brother, Bill, watched from the shadows of the den as his father performed his solemn task. After Ron was finished and stood back from the mantel, examining what he had just done, Bill clenched his teeth together and cleared his throat. His father turned.

"I got the mail," Bill said, motioning to the foyer.

"The mail?" Ron asked. He was wearing a weary, gray look on his face. Bill nodded toward the table in the foyer.

Stepping past his son and into the foyer, Ron picked up the mail and began sorting the envelopes. Bill watched his father's reflection in the oval mirror above the table. As Ron hunched over the mail, his bifocals slid down to the end of his nose.

"A card from Barbara," Ron said. He looked over his shoulder at Bill, holding the card up and waving it. Bill squeezed his lips together, attempting a smile.

"I'll bet you she wrote to say she won't make it to the memorial," his father said.

Bill shrugged his shoulders.

His father ran a pale hand over his shining forehead and turned back toward his son.

"She's that type, you know?"

"I know," Bill said.

"She's kinda nutty, isn't she?" Ron asked.

Bill shrugged his shoulders.

"She's always been that way. Ever since we were kids."

"Dad, I'm gonna go out …" Bill began.

"I called her Saturday," Ron said, cutting his son off. He looked at Bill with a helpless look.

"You called her?"

"Yes. You weren't here yet then. You were on the train, I think, by that time."

Bill nodded.

"God!" Ron shook his head. "I hated making those calls." He paused. Bill saw his father was squeezing the card so tightly it was bunching in a wrinkled mess. "Anyway," his father said, shaking his head. "She said then she'd try to make it."

He looked down at the crumpled envelope in his hands. He smiled to himself as he smoothed it out and tore open the back of it, pulling out the tattered card inside.

"She loved Terry, you know," Ron said without looking up.

"I know she did," Bill said.

"Those two just clicked for some reason," Ron continued. "I don't know what it was. Peas in a pod, I suppose."

"Peas in a pod?" Bill asked, frowning.

"Yes," Ron said, absently opening and closing the card in his hand without reading it. "They were so much alike. On some deep, primal level, you know? I think they were more alike than any of us will probably ever know." He nodded to himself. "She could at least make an effort to come."

He turned away from Bill again to read the card. A cold silence fell on the entry way as Bill approached the front door and leaned against it. In that position, he could no longer see his father's reflection in the mirror. Just then, the grandfather clock on the second floor landing chimed.

"No ..." Ron was shaking his head. "No. She isn't coming."

"Does she say why?" Bill asked, though at this point he didn't really care. He slipped his right hand into his pocket and felt the envelope he had put there before he came in the house with the mail.

"She's studying,'" Ron read. He looked at Bill over his shoulder. "In San Francisco."

Bill nodded. He moved the fingers in his pocket and felt the stamp on the envelope.

"'Studying,'" Ron huffed to himself and then chuckled, quick and loud. He closed the card, stuffed it back into the ripped envelope and turned to Bill, looking at him over the frames of his glasses. "'Zen Buddhism.' Whatever that is."

Bill shrugged his shoulders. Silence fell again. The pendulum of the clock on the landing swung in rhythmic humming clicks. Father and son looked uncomfortably at each other and then, together, they let their eyes falls to the floor.

"So," Bill finally said, breaking the uneasy silence. "Do you think Mom'll be alright?"

Ron Schwer nodded. "She'll be fine. She'll pull through."

"I haven't seen her at all today," Bill said, glancing up the stairs.

"The medication Doctor Netzler gave her is pretty strong, I guess," Ron said. "It's best if she gets as much rest as possible before tomorrow. She's still in shock, you know. She managed to go the funeral home with me to make the arrangements and, afterward, we went to St. Bart's to talk to the vicar about the memorial. But that night, she just crawled into bed and hasn't really been out since." He nodded for an unusually long time. Then, "She did come out, you know?"

"She came out of her room?" Bill asked, amazed.

Ron nodded.

"When?" Bill asked.

"Sometime last night," Ron said. "She ... uh ..." His voice trailed off. "She went into his room."

Bill frowned.

"I don't know why," Ron continued. "She was looking through his closet. Some of his clothes are still there, you know."

Bill nodded.

"Old hockey jerseys. Old sweaters and shirts. His sticks and pucks are in the back of the closet. He never took them with him when he moved out." He swallowed hard and loud. Then, "She went in there and just ... well, I don't know what she did. Maybe she just touched the clothes. Maybe she wanted to see if they still … smelled like him or not." He was looking at Bill's sneakers. "I don't know what she was doing in there." He nodded more. "And …"

"And …" Bill motioned impatiently for his father to continue.

"And …" Ron breathed deeply. "And she found an empty bottle of gin behind a suitcase."

Bill felt a sneer come up on his face.

"Terry's?"

"Who else's?" Ron shrugged. "It couldn't have been there long. We had all the rooms cleaned in April."

Bill felt his throat tighten.

"He came home and stayed the Memorial Day weekend, you know?" Ron asked.

"Yah, I knew that," Bill said.

"He had just finished finals. He told us they went well. He said he was acing everything. That was his word. 'Acing.'" Ron smiled. "Your mother and I knew something was wrong, though. We could sense it. We didn't know what it was exactly. We couldn't smell anything on him. He didn't even stumble or slur a word."

Bill shook his head. He let the fingers in his pocket tighten on the envelope.

"She didn't want you to know," Ron said.

"She didn't want me to know what?" Bill asked.

"About him. About … everything. She knows how much you idolize your brother."

Bill snorted with disgust.

"She didn't want you to know …" Ron started.

"To know what, Dad?" Bill exclaimed.

"She didn't want you to know how bad it really was."

"How bad it really was!" Bill shook his head. "Dad! I knew!"

"You knew?" Ron asked.

"I knew about his drinking even before you and Mom did. Do you honestly think he *just* started drinking?"

Ron opened his mouth but remained silent.

"Dad, he's been drinking since high school."

"Bill ..." Ron began.

"Why do you think he got kicked off the hockey team?"

Ron looked at his son with a sagging look of pity. "I ... I didn't know," his father said.

"I know you didn't," Bill said. "The coach covered it all up as long as he could. Terry knew how to cover it up so you and Mom never found out. He knew how to pull strings even then. He knew how to manipulate people and get them to do what he wanted them to do. That was his way."

Ron stared at his son in disbelief. "His way?"

"His way, Dad," Bill said. "His way of making sure he always came off shining and pure in your sight." He snorted with disgust. "I still don't know how he did it. He was just so ... so damned smooth and ..." Bill's voice trailed off into a grunt of frustration.

"What are you saying, Bill?" Ron asked.

"I'm saying, everyone knew," Bill said. "I'm saying it wasn't any secret except to you and Mom."

Ron's gaze dropped to the floor. "Oh, my God," he groaned. Then, looking at his son again, he asked, "How long has it been going on?"

Bill shrugged. "I don't know. Since high school. Maybe before that."

Ron continued shaking his head. "And *you* knew about this?"

Bill nodded.

"*You*? You knew?"

"Dad! I knew about it from the beginning. I always knew about it." The words came out of his mouth sounding more like an accusation than Bill intended. Immediately feeling remorse, he looked away from his father. After several moments of uneasy quiet, he looked back at Ron. His father was looking at the floor blankly, repeating his steady shaking movement with his head. When he stopped, he looked up at his son.

"Did he talk about *it*?" Ron asked. "Did he ever say anything ..."

Bill nodded. "Yes."

"He talked about ... the drinking?"

"Yes."

"When?"

"I visited him once," Bill said. "Right after I started college. He was living in the fraternity then. I think ..." He bit his lower lip.

"You think what?" Ron goaded.

"I think he'd been drinking for a long time before I got there."

"A long time? You mean non-stop?"

Bill nodded.

"How long is a long time?" Ron asked.

"A week maybe."

"A week straight?"

"I'd say," Bill said, nodding.

"Jesus," Ron muttered, shaking his head.

"I asked him right out. I said, 'How the hell long have you been drinking?'"

"And what did he say?"

"He said, 'Oh, there was just a killer party last night, that's all. Don't worry.'"

"Don't worry," Ron repeated sadly.

"But I called him on it. I said, 'Bullshit!' And that's when he cracked a little."

"He cracked a little? He talked to you about the drinking?" Ron asked.

"Yah. He said, 'You know something, Billy boy, I get this loudness inside my head.'"

"Loudness?"

"That's what he said."

"What did he mean?" Ron asked.

"I don't know," Bill replied. "But he went on. He said, 'Drinking's the only thing that *quiets* it.'"

"The loudness," Ron hissed.

"He said, 'Sometimes, Billy boy, it would be so much easier if I just ...'"

"No," Ron interrupted, holding up his hand. "I don't want to hear it."

"You asked," Bill said.

"I know," Ron said. "I know. But ... I just ... I don't want to hear it." His voice trailed off as his eyes fell to floor and stayed there.

Bill shifted his weight from one leg to another, feeling awkward, not knowing what to say. He rubbed his chin and felt the thick bristle of hair that grew there. He tried to remember the last time he shaved. The day before yesterday? he thought. Maybe the day before that? He couldn't remember.

Ron continued to look at the floor.

"Dad?" Bill said.

"Yes," Ron replied without looking at him.

"I'm going for a walk. I've got to get out of here."

"I don't blame you," Ron said, nodding. Then, after a pause. "Sure. You go. I'm going to read the paper." He lifted the folded newspaper and waved it in the air. "His obituary, you know."

"I know," Bill said, turning.

"He was so smart," his father said after a moment.

Bill's hand was on the knob of the door. The letter in his pocket felt hot and stiff against his leg. He closed and then opened his eyes once before turning around to face his father, who was looking at him with the same gray look he had only moments before.

"He was," Bill agreed.

"He was brilliant," Ron went on. "He had a mind like a puzzle. It was so ... intricate. I never understood what he was even saying half the time." He chuckled, but it was forced. It died easily in his mouth.

"Yah," Bill said, not knowing what else to say.

"If only ..." Ron said, trailing off.

"If only what?" Bill asked.

"If only he wouldn't have drank so much," Ron said. "I prayed."

"You prayed?" Bill asked.

"Oh, I prayed," Ron went on. "I prayed with all my heart. And your mother, too. We prayed that he's just ..."

"Prayer doesn't help," Bill said.

"How can you say that?" Ron asked, astonished.

"Look at how prayer didn't help." Bill motioned toward the canister on the mantle.

"If only he ..." Ron began before his voice trailed off again. "If only he could've just said something. If he could've just said *why*. That's all I want to know. Why?" His voice cracked.

Bill swallowed hard. The distance between his father and him seemed massive at that moment.

His father blinked away a wetness that shimmered in his eyes.

"Go," his father commanded. "Take that walk. It'll do you good."

Bill turned stiffly and slipped out the door without looking at his father again, carefully shutting it tight behind him. Only after he was off the porch steps and several feet onto the lawn did he dare inhale deeply. Letting the breath go, he felt at least temporarily cleansed.

The afternoon was clear and hot. There was a heavy smell in the fresh air—a sappy, pine smell. Sparrows trilled invisible in the trees around the house. Crickets hummed in the grass. Traffic on the highway down the wooded slope buzzed. From the front porch of the house, he could hear gears shifting. A horn sounded. After two days of oppressive silence, he was more keenly aware of the sounds outside the house than ever before. His head begin to throb as he felt the tension build of the sounds inside his skull.

He walked quickly around the side of the main house to a small greenhouse that stood just down the back lawn. He let himself in quietly and stood there, alone in the stifling heat, glancing around the interior. Adobe pots were neatly stacked on wooden shelves. There was a gritty, fertilizer smell in the air. He inhaled again, filling his nostrils with the pungent stink before reaching into his pocket and taking out the small envelope with large, scratchy writing.

Bill turned the small envelope over and over again in his hand. The stamp was upside down, there was no return address and his parents' house number was wrong. It was addressed simply SCHWER in block letters. The handwriting was like a child's, written in thick ink, stains here and there where the ink pooled. A smeared black thumbprint swirled above the envelope's fold. The fold itself was wrinkled like onionskin where too much spit had been used to seal it.

He looked around him at the pots and the wooden shelves and gritted his teeth. He picked at the sealed flap with his thumbnail. He bit his lower lip again, held his breath and carefully undid the back flap, pulling out the single sheet of notebook paper, its right edge fringed where it had been pulled from the wire-bound spine. There was writing on only one side of the sheet, and it was the same childlike scrawl as on the envelope. There were more black ink stains. Across the top of the page, his brother had absently drawn a streamer, two intersecting weaving lines. The letter was undated, though the post office bar stamped on the envelope was dated the day before. His brother had died the day before that. There was no greeting, nor was it addressed to anyone. It simply read, in almost bold scrawl:

Go to hell

Bill felt his stomach tighten.

Just those three words. No more. But those three words hit him with such force he felt as though he was going to lose his balance.

Bill bit his tongue until he felt a pain in the back of his throat. When he stopped biting, there was a sticky soreness in his mouth. He looked at the letter again, in absolute disbelief.

Go to hell

Bill felt nauseous and weak. He looked away, half-expecting that the words on the page would disappear. Or change. But there they were.

Go to hell

The only chair in the greenhouse was a splintering wooden lawn seat. Its red paint was flaking and its plats were cracked and rotten. Bill sat down just before the strength in his legs gave out. Only after he sat down did he see he had dropped the letter's envelope where he had been standing.

His palm was sweating and the sweat stained the paper in his hand. Bill worked his jaw back and forth until his teeth hurt.

"Jesus!" Bill exclaimed, looking up through the glass panes at the clear sky above.

He closed his eyes and turned his face back toward the paper in his hands. He took a deep breath, opened his eyes, and found the words glaring back at him:

Go
to
hell

Bill felt his upper lip curl at the image. The sneer was a hard one to relax. He was breathing heavily and beads of cold sweat formed on his forehead. His fingers actually ached as he held the paper. He felt a burning sensation flame through his knuckles.

As he looked closer at the three incriminating words, he realized there was no final punctuation. The sentence simply ended.

Bill released the letter and it fell into his lap. He leaned back against the upright of the lawn seat. Its rotting wood creaked under his weight. He felt it give a little and waited for it to break, but it held its own beneath him. He stared down blankly at the wooden floor. The envelope lay where he dropped it, face-down near a plastic sack of fertilizer. His gaze moved toward his feet. A movement suddenly caught his eyes and it took him a moment to recognize that a daddy long-legs was slowly crawling up his calf. He leaned over without thinking and flicked the spider into the half-light beneath the shelves.

His stomach churned and gurgled. He was almost afraid to move. He was sure if he did, he would vomit.

"Damn, Terry," Bill mumbled. "Damn *you*."

He had already torn the letter to pieces before he realized what he had done. He didn't even remember, a second afterward, that he had snatched the letter from his lap and cleanly tore it first in half, then a second time and finally a third. He looked at the torn pieces in his hands and then slowly let them fall to the dirty wooden floor. As he looked closely at the pieces, he saw one small paper shred with a single word on it:

hell

Bill stood up from the seat, picked up the envelope and quickly tore it to pieces, too. Then, dropping the pieces behind him, he went to the wall of windows that arced overhead. The greenhouse overlooked the back lawn, which sloped down toward the lake, hedged in on either side by thick woods. On the lake, there was a single white boat, its sail at full mast, slowly moving toward the north. Beyond the lake, he could just barely make out the thin, black steeple of St. Bartholomew's Episcopal Church.

Tomorrow, he thought to himself as he studied the needle-thin structure. *Tomorrow, Terry's ashes will be buried in the little cemetery behind that building.*

The pane he was looking though was cracked. He reached out and touched the familiar long, white sliver in the glass. This was the one Terry had flung a hockey puck against one January about five years before, Bill thought to himself.

No one hollered, Bill thought as he remembered that cold day out on the frozen lake. *No one said anything to you for that. You always got by with everything. Everything! Even* this!"

He stood back from the glass and suddenly caught his reflection in the pane. Although the reflection was distorted and split by the crack, he realized for the first time in his life how much he and Terry looked alike. The sunlight streaming down from overhead made long shadows in his eye sockets and beneath his chin. His pale skin looked ghostly and dead in the unmerciful light. His dark hair hung, loose and uncombed, in his face. It hadn't dawned on him until he looked at himself for some time that his mouth was hanging open in astonishment. Beads of cold sweat formed at his temples and ran down his cheeks, swathing his face in a wet shimmer.

"Damn," Bill hissed at the reflection staring back at him. "Terry! Damn, Terry!"

He reached down and picked up the first thing he found, a small hand trowel. Before he even knew what he had done, he hurled it at the cracked pane. The shattered glass showered outward onto the flower bed and the lawn beyond.

Bill stood in the middle of the greenhouse, breathing heavily. A single purple cloud moved, heavy and dark, overhead and temporarily blotted out the sunlight. A half-darkness fell over him as he exhaled deeply. He started to cry.

Inside the house, his mother quietly passed in and out of a drugged sleep upstairs in her bedroom. The moment the sound of the window in the greenhouse broke, she opened her eyes.

"Terry," she whispered quietly into her pillow. She then slowly allowed herself to be carried away by her barbiturate sleep.

Ron Schwer sat silently in the living room reading his son's obituary. He paused, buried his face in his hands and began sobbing just loud enough to cover the sound of the shattering glass in the green house.

His son's ashes sat alone, on the mantelpiece of the fireplace. When the sun finally broke through the purple cloud, one of its beams fell through the window of the den and settled on the plain tin box.

THE DOWNSTAIRS TENANT by Jamie Parsley

MRS. WENTWORTH'S AZALEAS

∎

The front page of Pinkham, North Dakota's, daily newspaper, *The Eagle,* for Tuesday, December 22, 1959, bore the headline: LOCAL NUN BEARS MYSTERIOUS WOUNDS. The full-page story went on to tell of how a twenty-four-year-old nun at the Sisters of Mt. Tabor convent awoke one morning the week before to a horrible pain in her wrists. "When she turned on the bedside light," the story read, "the young novice found her bed covered in her own blood and two holes, about an inch and a half in diameter, in each wrist. Two independent doctors were called to the convent to investigate and both reported that they could put their entire fingers into the wounds on Sister Bessier's wrists, although doing so caused the young novice much physical suffering."

From the time the story appeared until her death from leukemia at ten-thirty on Thursday morning, August 15, 1963, the young nun was hounded by pilgrims, skeptics, charlatans and the simply curious. A national Catholic newspaper in 1961 counted as many as five hundred pilgrims on the grounds in front of the Mt. Tabor Convent that year on the Feast of the Presentation, some of them traveling from as far away as England, the Belgian Congo and Goa, India.

The Tuesday before her death, she had asked if it was at all possible to go home to her parents' house to die. Much to the reluctance of the Superior of the convent and the Bishop of the diocese, the request was granted. Late that evening, Sister Mary of Jesus Crucified was bundled into the back of her father's station wagon and was whisked past the crowds of people who had gathered outside the convent's gates. On the day of her death, word spread quickly through the town that the nun had died at her parents' home on

Stockdale Drive on the west end of town. At noon, the bells of Immaculate Heart Catholic Church began tolling. By one o'clock that afternoon, the crowd, waiting for the hearse from the Durer-Zeitung Funeral Home to take her body away, had come together on the front lawn of the Bessier house on Stockdale Drive. By two fifteen, the mass of people was so thick it overflowed the Bessiers' lawn onto the lawn of Mrs. Althea Wentworth, the Bessiers' neighbor.

"Get off my lawn!" Mrs. Wentworth barked through her screen door the moment several of the people from the crowd were pushed across the invisible boundary between the two lawns. "Get off!" she hollered. "Look! Look what you're doing!"

The tall, thin, sharply featured woman motioned in front of her at her porch, where the sickly looking flowers grew around the brick basement foundation. "Do you see? Do you see what you're doing? You're stomping down my azaleas."

"We're not anywhere near your azaleas," a gnarled-looking woman in a turquoise, sleeveless dress and matching hat shouted back at Mrs. Wentworth. "We're just here to see them bring out the saint."

Mrs. Wentworth growled and threw open the screen door. In a moment, she had covered her front lawn with a stiff, determined stride and confronted the people nearest her house. Closer to the Bessier home, a hymn rippled through the people, quickly gaining strength:

Sing of Mary, pure and lowly
Virgin Mother, undefiled.

"Get out of here!" Mrs. Wentworth shouted over the singing. "Go on! All of you!"

The handful of spectators nearest the woman shifted together away from her as she waved at them madly.

Fairest child of fairest mother
God the Lord who came to earth, the crowd sang.

"Get off my damned lawn!" Mrs. Wentworth shouted.

"What are you saying?" a short man in shirt sleeves and black felt fedora gasped, putting a finger to his ear. His face was shiny with sweat. "I can't hear," he shouted over the singing. "I can't hear you!"

"I said!" Mrs. Wentworth screamed at him. "GET OFF MY DAMNED LAWN!"

The man gaped at her, wheezing.

Ave, Ave,

Ave Maria, the crowd continued.

"You too, Toots!" she screamed at a thin, elderly lady in a pink tulip-shaped hat.

The woman held a small, well-worn prayer book to her throat. "Well!" she exclaimed. "I've never!"

"Oh, I'm sure you haven't, honey," Mrs. Wentworth mumbled as she paced back and forth along her lawn, glaring at the people gathered there. Slowly, the music died away in the crowd and there was only the steady hum of almost a hundred people gathered together.

"So, what the hell's going on here?" Mrs. Wentworth barked at them as soon as the music finished.

"Don't you know?" a skinny teen-aged boy with greasy red hair asked. "The saint died. The hearse from the funeral home is coming to take her body away."

"Yes," a short, plain-faced woman dressed in a plaid bib-dress said. She held a chubby, expressionless baby to her breast. "She's a saint! A saint!"

"With the marks of her Lord on her hands!" the plain-faced woman's mother chimed in. She looked like an older, plumper version of her daughter. "On her *hands*! *Nail marks* on her *hands*! Have you *ever*!" she asked, stroking a growth of gray peach fuzz beneath her nose.

"What the hell are you talking about?" Mrs. Wentworth hissed. "A saint?"

"Sister Mary Stigmata!" a priest with bowed legs volunteered. He was fanning himself with a yellow, sweat-stained handkerchief.

"Sister Mary What?" Mrs. Wentworth hissed. She frowned so hard, the wrinkles on her forehead deepened into dark crisscrosses. "You're not talking about the Bessier girl?"

Several people in the crowd nodded.

Mrs. Wentworth snorted so loudly, the fat man in the fedora jumped.

"Ho-ho," Mrs. Wentworth chuckled. "You're one deceived bunch of idiots. Let me tell you something about your so-called 'saint.'"

"Do!" the bow-legged priest begged. He raised his folded hands, the sweaty handkerchief clutched in between, in her direction.

"Yes! Please!" the plain-faced woman's mother exclaimed.

"That little snot—that so-called saint, as you call her—well, ... oh, you're gonna love this—she used to *steal*. Yes! She'd steal my apples," Mrs. Wentworth instructed.

"No!" the teen-ager with the red hair hissed. "That can't be true!"

"You're damn right, she did. She used to sneak her saint-praying ass over here with all her snot-nosed brothers and sisters, and all of them—all ten of them—would just take them. Right off that tree."

"Which one?" the man in the fedora asked, looking around. "That one there?"

"How many apple trees do you see?' Mrs. Wentworth hissed. She nodded toward a tree near her house.

The crowd turned all together toward the tree. A nun in a white habit aimed a camera that hung around her neck at the tree and snapped three photos in quick succession.

"Oh, my God!" Mrs. Wentworth growled at the gap-mouthed crowd. "You *must* be joking!"

"The poor thing," two old ladies—identical except for the feathers they wore in their hats, one of peacock, one of ostrich—clicked in unison as they shook their heads at her. "She doesn't have an idea in her silly, old head, does she?"

"Get out!" Mrs. Wentworth shouted when she overheard them. "This is too much! I want you off my lawn. NOW!" She waved madly at the crowd as though they were a flock of chickens. "This is sick!" she continued. "Sick! You ghouls!"

"You don't understand," someone protested. Mrs. Wentworth looked about wildly at the group to see where it was the voice came from, but now all the voices jumbled in her ears and seemed to be coming at her from all directions.

"Oh, just go!" Mrs. Wentworth continued. "Get out. Get out!"

"She's got the Wound on her hands!" a priest in a long, black cassock and a shaking right hand shouted. "The Wound!"

"Yes! The Wound!" a woman with a salt-and pepper bouffant agreed. "The wound of Our Lord!"

"It gives off the smell of roses!" someone else shouted. Mrs. Wentworth was losing track of who was saying what.

"I don't care," Mrs. Wentworth shouted back. "She could be shitting pigeons for all I care. I just want you off my lawn!" She wiggled a gnarled finger at them, her liver spots glowing like tea stains on her skin.

"Hey, lady," a jowled man with a thick, black pompadour cut in. He nervously pulled at a bright yellow tie as he spoke. "You don't need to swear."

"Listen, I'm not gonna take etiquette lessons from you, Fat Boy," Mrs. Wentworth shot back. "This is *my* property." She scraped at her lawn with the toe of her scuffed penny loafer. "I can say any damned thing I want on *my* property. If I want to swear, I can. If want to strut around, naked as a centerfold, I can. *You*," she jabbed a finger in the fat man's direction," you don't tell me what to do or say. I don't kiss no toes. I'm no papist. Your rules don't apply to me. You understand that?"

She cast a cold, even gaze over the group.

"Ten minutes!" she hissed, holding up both hands, her fingers outstretched. "That's what I'm giving you. Ten minutes to get your mackerel-eating asses off my lawn or I'll have the cops here. And if you think I won't have them cart every one of you off to the can, you just go ahead and watch me. 'Cause I will. Oh, Christ, will I! So, keep it up, stupes, 'cause this party's coming to an end. Fast!"

And with that, she turned in a huff of air and stomped back across her lawn to her house. Before throwing open the screen door, she stopped and looked over her shoulder at the crowd. She raised a fist and shook it at them. "Stupes!" she screamed.

"Who was *that*?" the greasy-haired teenager asked no one in particular.

"*That* was Althea Wentworth," a skinny old man in a wrinkled suit, gray as an earthworm, answered.

The red-haired boy frowned.

"You've never heard of her?" the old man asked.

"No," the boy answered.

"Mrs. Wentworth?" The old man laughed. "Geez. I thought everyone had heard of her."

"So," the woman in tulip-shaped hat gasped, fanning herself with a holy card. "*That's* Mrs. Wentworth?"

"The *infamous* Mrs. Wentworth," the old man corrected.

"I read about her once in the newspaper," a young woman with a weak chin said.

"In the newspaper?" the red-haired boy asked. "Is she that famous?"

""Well, she's famous for getting herself in lots of trouble," the old man said. "There was this one time when she made the front page."

"Christmas Eve …" the woman with the weak chin cut in.

"… 1955," the two identical women chimed in together, finishing the young woman's sentence.

"What did she do?" the boy asked.

"What *didn't* she do?" the old man replied. "I still remember the headlines that next morning."

"Me, too," the young woman replied. "People around here still talk about *that*."

"It was right there on the front page of the Christmas Day edition," the old man continued. "Right under 'A Visit from St. Nick.' LOCAL WIDOW GOES ON X-MAS EVE RAMPAGE."

"What did she do?" the boy asked.

By this time the crowd had tightened around the old man, waiting for what he had to say next.

"She pelted Holy Innocents Episcopal Church with her own homegrown squash," the old man said.

"And those purple onions she grows in her backyard in the summer," the two old women with feathered hats sang in unison.

"And a whole carton of eggs," the old man continued. "And she did it right there in broad daylight."

"In full view of the police station across the street," the young woman piped in.

"She was arrested, right?" the boy asked.

"Oh sure," the old man said. "Ol' Sheriff Clickfield hauled her off right quick. But not before she knocked the head off the nativity scene's Virgin Mary.

"I'm sure sacrilege like that means nothing to *her*," the woman in the tulip-shaped hat said, nervously fumbling with her lamé purse.

"It was like shooting bottles off a fence for her," the old man said.

"Why'd she do it?" the man in the fedora asked.

"She told the police she was 'justified,'" the old man replied.

"Justified?" the woman in the tulip-shaped hat exclaimed. "How you can be justified committing sacrilege on devout Christians?"

"She said it was in retaliation for an 'unmitigated attack' — those are her exact words, as I remember them—on her private property by the church's St. Monica's Guild, who had approached her house the day before seeking donation for their Indo-Chinese Children's Fund." The old man paused, shaking his head. "After chasing them off her porch with a cane that had belonged to the late Mr. Wentworth, she called Sheriff Clickfield to tell him to arrest the St. Monica's Guild for trespassing. When he refused, I guess she just decided to take the law into her own hands."

The red-haired boy looked on with an amazed expression on his face.

"Wicked!" a woman in a black mantilla sobbed. "It's just wicked the evil that is present among us!"

"What makes a woman turn so evil?" the woman with the gray mustache asked.

"Well, you know, ol' Althea, she wasn't always so bad," the old man said. "No. Like most people, there was a time when she was different. Or at least, there was a time when she wasn't *as* bad."

"How would *you* know?" the red-haired boy asked.

"'Cause I knew the late Mr. Wentworth," the old man replied.

"Really?" the boy asked.

"Oh, yah. Ol' Vic Wentworth and I went back to before the Great War. He and I went to high school together. And then we joined the Army together, 'cept I got sent to a camp in Michigan to cook food and he got sent to France, where he was gassed."

"What was he like, this Mr. Wentworth?" the chubby woman with the plain-faced baby asked.

"Vic? Oh, he was real quiet. Kinda shy, you know. But he was a good guy, that Vic. No, you woulda' never thought he'd 'a got himself mixed up with the likes of Althea Wentworth. In fact, no one thought ol' Vic would ever get hitched. I mean, we musta' been back from the war about twenty years and he hadn't even batted an eye at any one in all that time. 'Course no one thought anything of it. He was pretty messed up in the war. We all thought some of that Hun gas got into his brain somewhere and kinda messed him up. But sure enough, when Althea came wiggling into town one day with her mother and brother, ol' Vic, he just fell head over heels for her."

"Wow!" the boy exclaimed. "I woulda' never guessed it from *her*!"

"Oh, yah," the old man went on. "She was a looker. Ol' Vic kept saying, 'Lookit her! She looks just like Carole Lombard!'"

"Carole Lombard!" the woman with the salt-and-pepper bouffant exclaimed.

"*That* wrinkled old thing!" the woman in the tulip-hat asked, crooking her thumb toward Mrs. Wentworth's house.

"Oh, yah, she was quite a looker, you know. Now, I wouldn't say she was any Carole Lombard. But she sure wasn't bad. Obviously, she wasn't bad."

"What do you mean by that?" the boy asked.

"Well, you see, Althea's mom was a widow, you know. She came into town about twenty, twenty-five years ago with Althea and this deaf and dumb son of hers and opened up a boarding house on the south side of town, right across from the depot. Althea's mom pretty much just put up guys that were stoppin' off on their way through, following the trains wherever they went. Well, ol' Vic, he told me that Althea couldn't stand living in that place. The mother, she had enough to do, taking care of the house and bedding and all. And the boy, well, I don't think he ever did anything but sit in his room all the time. Poor Althea was cooking all the meals and serving them to these guys. And, of course, all these lonely guys having Carole Lombard serving them their meals, well, I'm sure they were pawing at her left and right. I think she was just looking for any escape from that place. And so, when ol' Vic popped the question, she was more than willing to say 'I do!'"

"Were they happy, Althea and ol' Vic?" the boy asked.

"I don't know," the old man said. "I met her only once and that was after they got hitched. She seemed civil. I mean, she'd carry on a conversation just as normal as can be. 'Course, you could tell there was something wrong there. You saw it in her eyes. This … I don't know what you'd call it. Anger. Bitterness. Like an animal backed into a corner. You know what I mean? Anyway, she bossed poor Vic around. And pretty soon, I just saw less and less of him."

"He'd dead, then?" the boy asked.

"Oh, yah," the old man said. "He died in about 1948. I saw him once more about a month or two before he died on East Bank Street, at the Piggly Wiggly, carrying out groceries to the car. She never did the grocery shopping. She had him do it all the time. The poor guy! He had the look of a beaten dog on him. Of course, he never said anything about what his life had been like in those ten years. But you know, just between us, I sometimes wonder if ol'

Vic didn't wish once or twice that it would've been ol' Althea who went down on that airplane and not Carole Lombard. You know what I mean? Anyway, it wasn't long after that I read in the paper that Vic had died, of a heart attack, I heard, and that's when Althea went completely over the deep end."

"You mean she wasn't like that before he died?" the boy asked.

"Oh, I'm sure she was," the old man said. "But after Vic died, it just became more ..." he struggled for the word. "It became more *obvious*. She just went completely batty. She didn't leave the house for weeks on end. And when she did, she'd look all wild-eyed, her hair a mess. She looked like a witch or something. You know how things like that get around, especially in a town this size. Before you could blink, everyone was calling her that. 'Witch! Witch!' That's all you'd ever hear whenever you'd see her walking down the street. 'Lookit the witch. Lookit her.' You can't blame them, really. You saw what she looks like now. She *does* look like a witch. It was sad, though, seeing little kids clutch their mothers when ol' Althea would stand glaring at them in the Piggly Wiggly.

And then, of course, there was Halloween. That was a terrible time. Some little group of punks would always test their guts by sneaking in her backyard to tap on her window screens or egg her house. Oh, Lord! You should've seen the fury that woman would go into over that! You could hear her screaming two, three blocks away. Her screaming, and those kids laughing as they ran from her yard. I honestly think something snapped in the ol' girl when ol' Vic died. She just turned angry at everyone and everything. And you know, she had something special in her craw concerning religion."

"Why is that?" the bow-legged priest asked.

"I don't know," the old man said. "I heard somewhere — I don't even remember now where I heard this — that Althea's dad has been one of those traveling preachers. You know the ones. They'd go from town to town with their tents and their crank organs, preaching fire and brimstone. Anyway, the story went around for a while that her dad had been shot in a hotel room in Iowa or Wisconsin or someplace when one of his parishioners caught him there in bed. In the arms of the other guy's wife, see? It was such a scandal in its day, that's part of the reason Althea and her mother and brother moved up here. The way I have it figured, I don't think she ever forgave her preacher-dad for dying on her the way he did. But, mind you, that's just my thinking."

The old man stood quietly for a moment. He made a clicking sound with his mouth as he let his eyes fall to the ground. Around him, the crowd shook their heads quietly.

"Stop that!"

The sound cut through the warm summer air like a shotgun blast. It was so loud, one or two people looked up to the sky to see if a bomb had dropped. But most everyone else recognized the voice and turned their heads toward Mrs. Wentworth's house.

"Stop it! Stop it right this minute!"

Mrs. Wentworth was off her front porch and half-way across her front lawn before the screen door slammed shut behind her. She was pointing at the man in the fedora, who was slowly exhaling gray smoke rings into the air.

"Who, me?" the man asked when he realized he was on the receiving end of Mrs. Wentworth's fury.

"Yes, *YOU*!" Mrs. Wentworth screamed, motioning at his cigarette. "Stop *that*! Stop flicking those damned ashes on my lawn."

"I wasn't," the man stammered.

"You were!" Mrs. Wentworth shot back. "I saw you! I was watching you from my window!"

The crowd closer to the Bessier house decided at that moment to begin singing another hymn. Quickly the singing spread among the group, gaining pitch and precision, and Mrs. Wentworth's voice was drowned out.

> *For all the saints, who from their labors rest,* the crowd sang.
> *Who thee ... by faith before the world confessed.*

Throughout the hymn, Mrs. Wentworth's mouth moved, but no one heard the steady string of profanities she was casting in the direction of the people closest to her.

> *Thy name, O Jesus,*
> *be forever blessed*, the crowd continued singing,
> *Alleluia,*
> *alleluia!*

As she ranted, Mrs. Wentworth stomped her feet and pulled her iron-gray hair from its loosely wound bun. She swayed in a circle on her front lawn and tore at her cardigan and housedress. She kicked at the open air and as she did, she flung the brown penny loafer from her left foot, and it arced through the air, nearly hitting the woman with tulip-shaped hat. The man in the fedora had, in the meanwhile, quickly crushed out his cigarette beneath the sole of one of his black wing-tips.

Thou wast their rock, the crowd sang.
Their fortress and their might,
Thou, Lord, their captain in the well-fought fight.

As the hymn slowly died away, Mrs. Wentworth stood, panting and sweating, on the edge of her lawn. Her hair was wild and loose around her long, drawn face.

"Fanatics!" she screamed. "I warned you! Singing your damned hymns. Bastards! All of you. Every last one of you! Damn! Fanatics!"

The nun with the camera raised her hands to the sides of her head, covering her ears, and squeezed her face as Mrs. Wentworth cursed.

"You asked for it!" Mrs. Wentworth continued. "Every one of you! You asked for it! I hope you're all happy! I hope every one of you got a little peck at that dead girl's corpse—Peck! Peck! Peck!—because this is it! This is the end! I'm not gonna take any more. No more! I'm gonna call the cops! I'm gonna sit up there on my damned porch and laugh! I'll laugh as they drag every last one of you sons-of-bitches off to the lockup! I'll laugh and laugh! You watch!"

"Now listen here!" someone from the back of the crowd protested. "We don't need to take this from you!"

But Mrs. Wentworth was no longer listening. "I don't understand you people!" she screamed. "Look at yourselves. Just look! Look what you're doing! Am I the only one who sees it? Don't *you* see it?" She pointed at the old man in the wrinkled gray suit. "Don't any of you *see*? Vultures! That's what you are! You're all a bunch of vultures! You're standing around here waiting for them to bring out a dead nun with cuts on her hands. Am I the only one who sees how sad and desperate that is?"

She turned on the heel of her one remaining shoe. As she did, she suddenly felt a shot of electric pain shoot down the inside of her left arm. "Fanatics!" she cursed as she gasped at the pain. Another bolt of pain shot down her arm and this time she gasped one word, sharp as a knife cut, "Oh!"

Immediately she felt a numbness pour through her body. This was followed by yet another shiver of pain. As the numbness coursed through her body, she felt her legs give out beneath her weight. She staggered, gasping for air, toward the nearby apple tree and fell against it. Her back against the tree, she slowly slid down toward the lawn. As she settled onto the grass amid a scattering of fallen, half-rotten apples, her dentures fell from her mouth, frothy with spittle. There she sat, one shoe on, one shoe off, her housedress hiked over knees, her stockings bunched down at her ankles.

"Oh … god … god … da … da …" Mrs. Wentworth hissed.

Another volt of pain shot through her body. Pinpricks of blue and white light played in her eyes. Her breath was sucked out of her chest, her body tensing with the pain. A tightness formed in her throat.

"What's happening to her?" a little girl in pigtails and a lazy brown eye asked.

"She's collapsed!" the man in the black fedora exclaimed, crossing from the Bessiers' lawn to Mrs. Wentworth's apple tree. He approached the gasping old woman cautiously, holding back as he leaned over her, as though he were afraid she might leap up at him and bite him on one bony thigh.

"God …" Mrs. Wentworth gasped again as she sat, bolt-upright against the apple tree, staring off into nothingness. "… God … da … god … da …" Her right hand clutched at her chest, her floral housedress bunching in a knot in her fist.

"What did she say?" the red-haired teen-age boy asked the woman with the tulip-shaped hat as they slowly walked together toward the tree.

"Did I hear her right?" the woman with the weak chin asked. "Did she call out for God?"

"I think so," the woman in the black mantilla exclaimed. "I'm sure I heard her call out 'God!' She said it! 'God!'"

Mrs. Wentworth sat against base of the apple tree, staring off blankly, sputtering and gasping to herself. Her left hand was clenching and releasing grass, soil and rotten apples beside her.

"… God … da … God … da …"she mumbled toothlessly.

"She *is*!" the woman in the tulip-hat shouted. "She *is*! She *is*! She's calling out to the Lord!"

"Thank you, Sister Mary Stigmata!" the woman with the salt-and-pepper bouffant rejoiced. She clutched a rosary to her chest as she looked up into the heavens with a rapturous expression.

"A miracle!" a tall, wide-shouldered boy with an uneven blond crew-cut cried. He made a sign of the cross over a red and white T-shirt that read STILSON HIGH SCHOOL SENTINALS.

"Mrs. Wentworth's converted!" a tall man with a single thick, black eyebrow shouted to those still on the Bessiers' lawn. Those around him strained forward, standing on their toes to catch a glimpse of the dying woman beneath the apple tree. "Come over!" the tall man shouted to the rest of crowd, clapping his hands with wild abandon. "Come! Come and see the miracle!"

"God … God … da … mn … you …"Mrs. Wentworth struggled as her lips turned blue. But no one heard her. The crowd gathered around her, shouting praises into the sky.

The nun in the white habit stepped forward and looked down into the camera she held. She quickly snapped off three photos of Mrs. Wentworth's grimacing, toothless face.

"A miracle!" the nun grinned as she looked up from the camera. "A miracle! I just can't believe it!"

Mrs. Wentworth's eyes rolled back into their sockets until they finally fixed on a low-hanging branch in the tree above her. The apples there swayed heavily in the breeze. The muddy toes on her shoeless left foot curled inside the bunched-together stocking. Her sod-filled fingers refused to unclench and release the torn grass her fingers had torn up. The last thing she smelled before the darkness overtook her was the stench of rotting apples and, further away, the slightly more pleasant odor of azaleas in the air.

THE DOWNSTAIRS TENANT by Jamie Parsley

MUNDA COR MEUM

∎

1.

The beads were large and round and black, and Brian felt a strange excitement as he rolled them back and forth between forefinger and thumb.

"An early Christmas present," his mother said when she let him open the gift. Not that it was a gift she would ever have thought of giving her eleven-year-old Lutheran son. But he had been asking for the rosary for months, ever since his strange interest became more and more intense.

Before heading to the Catholic religious supply store downtown to purchase the rosary, she first talked to Father Atkins, rector at Grace Episcopal Church.

"Don't worry," he assured her. "It's just a phase. It will pass. Kids are sometimes curious about other religions. Once he figures out that we're as Catholic as the Romans, he might very well embrace his own faith."

"I don't like it," her husband told her as she wrapped the present. "Does he even know what they are?"

"He's been begging for them for months," she said. "Besides, considering how he hates going to these family get-togethers at your parents' place every Christmas, this may just pacify him."

"I hope so," her husband said. "But, I'll say it again. I just don't like it."

After opening the present and drawing out the long rosary, Brian glowed as he sat on his bed. It was exactly how he imagined they looked, though he never realized how wonderful it was to hear the sounds the beads made when they came out of the box.

"Maybe this will make the get-together at grandma and grandpa's a little better," his mother said.

"It will!" Brian said, though even as he said it, he wasn't all that sure. But even that did not matter. Not now. He couldn't wait to say the beads for the first time.

"I still am not pleased with this," his father announced. "And I don't understand any of this." He waved his hand around Brian's room, in which the boy had placed small plastic statues of different saints he found at rummage sales and in second-hand stores. A large, framed, badly painted portrait of the Virgin Mary holding her heart in her hand, red as an apple, hung above the boy's bed.

But Brian's excitement and his enthusiastic gratitude at least temporarily undid his parents' disappointment.

After his parents left the room, Brian closed the door and took out a small, black, worn book. The cover of the book read THE ST. ALOYSIOUS DAILY MISSAL. He found the book at an old woman's garage sale early the previous summer. Inside the cover was the name of who Brian assumed was her son, and it seemed as though the book had never been opened. He now flipped through the pages he himself had wrinkled with use and found the section titled HOW TO PRAY THE ROSARY, illustrated with pastel illustrations of events from the life of Jesus. Reading the instructions, he carefully kissed the crucifix on the rosary, made an awkward and possibly incorrect sign of the cross and began the Creed.

2.

Brian's boy-cousins were farm kids. They even looked like farm kids; wide shoulders, like quarterbacks; sun-burned faces; dirty knuckles the size of quarters. And what always amazed Brian the most was the fact they all had hair on their chests by the time they were twelve. They'd unbutton the top two or three buttons and comb the stiff hairs with their fingers until they folded over the edge of the cloth.

And they were thick-tongued, every one of them, speaking in a hybrid German-Norwegian accent that he occasionally was unable to understand.

Certainly the last things those boys ever understood were toys. Not even their only sister for that matter. Poor Alvina—tall, thick-hipped and gawky in her cotton prints—never played with dolls or makeup. She just stood off to the side while her brothers pushed themselves around and everyone else who got in their way. Those kids never needed toys, after all. Their parents—larger, more fierce version of their children—made no secret of what they expected from their offspring.

Brian's mother told him one time about what Aunt Thelma announced to her one Easter as the whole family was gathered at his grandparents' house. "We made it perfectly clear," Aunt Thelma said.

"Perfectly clear," Uncle Knut cut in, nodding.

"We promised each other the day the first of those kids were born that they were gonna work the farm the day they learned to walk."

"No need to baby them," Knut said.

"Certainly not!" Thelma said.

"Nothing's free, you know?" Knut said.

"It sure isn't," Thelma agreed. "If they can walk …"

"… they should work," Knut finished.

"Damn straight," Thelma agreed.

And that, as far as anyone who might have doubted them was concerned, settled the matter once and for all.

Still, Brian always found the whole situation so unthinkable. He understood that, although they didn't have toys, they certainly had animals. Animals, mind you. Not *pets*. They were never considered pets. The huge, barking yard dog—if he remembered it correctly, was simply named Mutt—was a watch dog. The tomcats that prowled the granaries and barns kept the rodent population down. Cows and fowl were produce and 4-H awards. Instead of toy cars and model airplanes, his cousins fixed combines and car engines. More often than not *just for fun*.

It was these cousins Brian dreaded more than anything. And on this particular Christmas, as he went with his parents to his grandparents' farm house with the brand-new black-beaded rosary jangling in his pocket, he felt fortified. When he first saw the cousins as he entered the house, he reached in his pocket and, feeling the cool beads there, he felt strangely calm.

He ignored the snickers behind his back until, bored by festivities, he made his way down into the dark, nearly empty root cellar beneath the house, where he had planned on praying another section of his new rosary, if only he could remember the prayers he only just learned. It was there his boy-cousins cornered him.

"Lookee there!" Kai, the oldest of them, mocked. "Have we stumbled upon a little Bible study down here?" Kai proceeded to pull the rosary from Brian's hands. "Jee-zuz!" Kai growled. "Look at this! What is this? A necklace? Oh, Floyd, you'd look positively gorgeous with this around your neck."

"Shaddup," Floyd barked. Floyd was the second oldest and was by far the heaviest of all the boys. His bloated stomach hung in a soft roll over the waist of his blue jeans. "So, Holy Joe," Floyd said, turning his attention back to Brian. "Where do you get your necklace, then? Huh?"

"Yah," Kai growled. "Where'd you git it?'

"It's one of those Cathlick necklaces, isn't it? Are you a Cathlick now, Holy Joe? Is there some sort of Cathlick store in the city where boys like you can git themselves Cathlick necklaces to wear like this one here?" Floyd asked.

"There has to be," Kai said. "One Cathlick store on every Cathlick street."

"You know what Cathlicks do?" Lyle asked Kai.

"Wear necklaces?" Kai asked.

"Yah, they do that, too. But you know what else they do? They drink blood."

There was a shocked silence in the basement.

"What are you talking about," Alvina piped up.

"Cathlicks drink blood," Lyle said. "I heard about it once. They do all these secret things in their churches and drink real blood."

"They don't drink blood," Floyd said, though his voice betrayed his uncertainty.

"Yes, they do," Lyle said. "I heard it."

"Is that why you're liking all this Cathlick crap?" Kai asked Brian. "Huh? You turning into some kind of vampire? Is that it?"

"Are you a vampire?" Lyle taunted.

The other two boys—Lyle and Tom—and big-boned Alvina cackled near the stairs they blocked. Slowly they moved together in a tight half-circle around him. As they did, he felt a by-now familiar feeling come into his stomach, tight and sour.

"Come on, guys," he said, trying to negotiate his way out of the situation that he knew would get worse before it got better. "Just let me go back upstairs. Please."

"No," Kai hissed. "I don't think so. I think we want to have a little fun here with you and your little necklace here. And if you don't like that, Holy Joe, you sure go ahead and try and do something about it."

"Yah, Pope," Floyd cut in. "Go ahead. I'd really like to see what you can do."

He was breathing heavily by this point. The tightness that had come into his stomach seemed to be cutting off his breathing. Besides, he couldn't believe how huge they all seemed. Wide shoulders. Thick, long legs. Dirty blond hair. And as they moved closer toward him, he was sure he smelled a mixture of hay, manure and axle grease.

"Come on, Pope," Kai taunted, swinging the rosary in front of his face by the crucifix. "No?" he asked. "You're not even gonna try? OK." He nodded and let go a chortle that sent a chill up and down Brian's spine. "Heads up, Lyle," Kai said as he tossed the rosary over his shoulder to Lyle, who caught it with a fumble.

"Ohhh, wheee!" Lyle hissed, holding it up and admiring it like it was full of diamonds. "I've never seen such a pretty thing in all my life. I betcha you'll fight for this pretty thing, won't you, Pope. I've never seen a boy like you fight before. So, come on. I wanna see you fight."

"I don't fight," Brian pleaded. "Just give it to me!"

"'Just give it to me,'" Lyle mimicked.

"No!" Floyd said, snatching the rosary from Lyle and swinging it over Brian's head. "No begging! If you want it, you fight for it. Come on, Holy Joe. You can do it. Fight!"

"It's not that hard," Kai cut in. "All you gotta do is make a fist and just come out swinging." He brought up his hand with a sudden movement, making Brian flinch. As he did, his cousins all laughed. "Now, watch," Kai said as he held his hand in front of Brian's face. He pointed his thumb straight up. Then he wrapped the other fingers on his hand around the thumb, making a huge fist. "Now that's how weak little boys like you make a fist. When you fight, you make a fist like that." Brian's cousins laughed again.

"Ah, boys like you can't fight," Lyle mocked. "You only know how to play with necklaces. Pretty, Cathlick necklaces."

"Just give it back," Brian repeated. The lack of air going to his head made him feel suddenly very light-headed. He knew if this kept up much longer, he would either vomit or cry. Either option would not help the situation at all. Finally, in a last ditch effort, he resorted to the only option he knew he had. "Listen, guys," he said. "If you don't give it back to me right now …"

"Ah, cripes," Alvina hissed, looking nervously back up the stairs. "This is getting boring. Just give him back his stupid necklace."

"Yah," Tom agreed. "Let's just go back upstairs before we get in trouble."

"Shut up!" Kai growled at his brother and sister. "Both of you just shut your mouths." He then turned his attention back to Brian. "Give it to me, Lyle," Kai commanded through clenched teeth. Lyle handed the rosary over. Kai dangled it in front of Brian's face by the upside down crucifix. Brian couldn't, for whatever reason, look Kai straight-on and so he found himself turning away from Kai, looking at him instead with a side-long glance. One side of Kai's mouth slowly curled into a sneer. "OK, Pope," Kai said. "I don't know who you think you are. Ever since you were little, you came here thinking you were something."

"You are something," Lyle hissed. "Something strange!"

"No, you're not," Kai hissed. "You and all your goody-goody ways. Walking around like some kind of …" he struggled to find the words

"Like some kind of Holy Joe," Lyle said.

"Yah, like some Holy Joe," Kai said. "Everyone thinks you're so good. You're just …" again he struggled, but this time Kyle didn't add anything. When Kai glanced at Lyle, he just shrugged. Finally, Kai glared back at Brian. "You're nothing. You're just a weak, little sniveling little pansy who likes to wear Cathlick necklaces. That's all. So here." He dangled the rosary in front of Brian's face.

"We wouldn't want you to throw a conniption or anything. Just go! Go back your mommy and daddy."

"Yah," Floyd added. "Just go back to Cathlicktown."

Kai stared Brian down with a hard, gray look for a long moment before he simply released his thumb and forefinger. The rosary fell to the floor. Brian stepped back and looked at it lying at his feet. For a moment, he didn't know what to do. He was too afraid to move. After looking in the faces that surrounded him, cautiously, hesitantly, he bent at the knees and carefully reached to pick it up. It was then that Kai, suddenly and without warning, swung and punched him in the upper arm. The hollow thud resounded through the basement as his fist connected with Brian's arm. In an instant, he saw a blinding white sliver in his vision. The shock of the blow caused Brian to lose his balance and he fell to the floor. As he did, his cousins all laughed. They were still laughing as they left him where he was on the cold, dirty pavement of the basement floor, rubbing his arm and trying desperately to hold back his tears.

Brian picked up the rosary from the floor and, straightening up, he watched his cousins mount the creaking steps. As he saw their turned-away backs and listened to their derisive chuckling, he felt another flash of white light in his mind.

"Supra quae prpitio ac sereno vultu respicere digneris," Brian pronounced, both shocked at what was coming from his mouth and uncertain if what he was saying was pronounced correctly.

His cousins stopped on the stairs and turned around in shock. Kai's face was contorted in confusion.

"What did he say?" Lyle asked. "What was that?"

"Et accepta habere, sicuti accepta habere dignatus et mudera pueri tui justi Abel," Brian continued.

The cousins stood there in shocked silence as Brian's voice grew bolder.

"What is he saying?" Lyle asked again, his voice more desperate than before.

"Et sacrificium Patriarchae, nostri Abrahae: et quod tibi obtulit summus sacerdos tuus Melchisedech." No one was more shocked and surprised than Brian. Where was this coming from? he wondered as the words poured from.

The cousins on the stairs slowly started moving backward up the stairs as they looked at Brian in shock and, deeper down in their eyes, a growing fear.

"… sanctum sacrificium …" Brian continued as he moved toward them. As he did so, they moved more furtively away from him. "… immaculatam hostiam."

By the time, Brian reached the stairs, the cousins were scrambling up and out of the basement, almost tumbling over themselves as they went. The last of them to climb from the basement was Kai. He paused and looked at Brian.

"This is not over, Pope," he hissed.

Brian had one foot on the bottom step as he looked up at Kai, the rosary swinging tightly from his right hand as he stood there.

"Sanctum sacrficium," Brian repeated. "… immaculatam hostiam."

Kai's lips tightened as he stumbled on the last step and disappeared around the door post.

Brian stood at the bottom step, breathing heavily. Sweat broke out on his forehead at some point and his face was suddenly drenched.

"Amen," he said to himself, as he tucked the rosary in his pocket. He took one more deep breath. As he did, he felt himself smile. His lips stiffened and grew hard against his face.

"Amen," he repeated to himself. And then, slowly, he ascended the stairs.

FROM AMIDST THE WIND

■

1.

Like a freight train.

Margaret had heard once that's what a tornado would sound like when it came through. But now, as it was actually plowing through the city, she thought it sounded more like someone was moving a large dresser or trunk across the floor upstairs. Or maybe a truck speeding by on the street in front of her house at full speed. She put her hands to her ears and closed her eyes, hoping it would simply blow itself out quickly.

"Don't worry, Mom," Dennis told her as he stood, tall and skinny in the middle of the basement with his Bible clutched to his thin chest. "It's just the angel of death going over. But I heard the word of Lord and He told …"

"… He did not," Lorlene interrupted.

"He did so!" he snapped at his sister. He then turned his attention back to his mother. "He told me to put blood on the door sill. And I did. Wren's blood."

"Denny!" his mother complained.

"'Denny,'" Lorlene mimicked her mother's voice.

"It's all right, Mom," Denny said. "He'll pass by and let us be. You'll see."

"I don't want you doing that anymore," Margaret said, holding up a finger to him. "No more animal's blood anywhere. OK."

"But the Lord …" Dennis began.

"No more animal blood!" she said firmly.

The boy's face tensed but he was quiet.

"Not you go sit over there in the corner by your sister."

Lorlene was huddled beneath the wringer washer on the wall opposite her mother. As the tornado came closer and closer and the deep, steady rumbling grew louder, the little girl's face lengthened, becoming skinny with agitation. The air in the basement seemed to thin, and as it did, the little girl's eyes widened and her mouth opened into a perfectly round black O. The sound grew louder, the girl's mouth grew wider and her pupils rolled back so far into her skull, only the whites of her eyes could be seen.

Dennis sat down beside the washer and bowed his head into the large Bible perched on his knees front of him. He began praying quietly to himself.

At one point Margaret looked up through the small window high on the basement's cement wall and saw the black cloud moving against the gray sky behind it. Boards and shingles circled each other in the blackness high up in the sky.

And then after almost five minutes, with a whistling sigh, it was done. Margaret sat on the cold basement floor, her back against the wall, looking up through the window. Slowly she saw the gray sky lighten. Still she did not move.

"Mom …?" Dennis began.

"Shhh!" Margaret hissed, putting a finger to her lips.

The heavy silence that followed the tornado was quickly followed by a steady, rhythmic sound.

"It's raining!" Dennis called across the room to her. Beside him, Lorlene, resuming her usual, slightly blank-eyed expression, smiled at her mother from beneath the thick legs of the washer.

"See!" Dennis shouted. "See! I told you! The angel of the Lord passed over and spared our home."

"Dennis," his mother intoned.

"'Dennis,'" Lorlene repeated, grabbing at Dennis' red plaid shirt playfully.

"No, Mom. Listen. It's the blood that did it." He stood up, hugging his big Bible.

Margaret breathed deeply in and out quietly as she watched her son cross the basement.

"You can thank me later," he said to Margaret as he climbed the steps out of the basement.

2.

The tornado hit at four ten that Wednesday afternoon. The telephones were out until seven. Margaret jumped when the phone finally rattled to life at seven fifteen.

"Is everyone there all right?" her sister Maureen exclaimed on the other line.

"Everything's fine," Margaret said. "The only damage was a couple of shingles pulled off the roof and an overturned pot of marigolds on the front porch. There were two roofs blown off on the street just behind our house."

"And Pete? What about Pete?" Maureen exclaimed.

"Pete's on business in Minneapolis," Margaret said. "He probably hasn't even heard about the storm yet. So, how about you? Everyone all right there?"

"Everything's fine here," Maureen said quickly. "Though it sounds like you haven't heard about Alice, then?"

"Alice?" Margaret asked, frowning. "Alice who?"

"*Cousin* Alice!" Maureen exclaimed.

"What about her?"

"Like a soup can," she heard her brother-in-law, Mark, intoning in the background.

"Will you shut up?" Maureen yelled to Mark.

"What about Alice?" Margaret asked.

"They found Alice and Kevin. They weren't so lucky."

"Like a soup can. Like a damned soup can," Mark was intoning between sobs.

"Mark and a couple of other workers from the city found Alice and Kevin's Plymouth about three blocks from their house. He said it was all crumpled up …"

"… like a soup can," Mark was murmuring.

"Yah, yah, all right," Maureen ticked impatiently back to him. Then, "It was a real wreck, anyway. The trunk was sprung. The windshield was shattered. When they looked inside to see if there was anyone in there, they pulled him out."

"Kevin?" Margaret asked.

"Kevin," Maureen said. "Mark said when they pulled Kevin out, his hair was white. White. Can you imagine? Twenty-seven years old and his hair was *white*."

"White as cotton," Mark sobbed in the background.

"He didn't even know it was Kevin," Maureen said.

"Well, Christ," the woman heard Mark moan. "How the hell was I supposed to know it was him with that white hair? It was only when we laid him out on the sidewalk and the rain started washing the blood away that I …" His voice broke off in sobs.

"They found Alice a half a block away. Her eye was knocked out," Maureen intoned.

"They're dead," Margaret said quietly.

"Who's dead?" Dennis said, suddenly appearing behind her with his Bible in one hand. He was tugging at her skirt.

"Go in the other room," Margaret hissed at her son, holding a hand over the mouthpiece of the phone. Dennis squeezed his face at her and, with a stomp, huffed off into the kitchen.

"Imagine!" Maureen went on. "Only three blocks from their house. And their house. I guess it wasn't even damaged."

Their house. Margaret had never seen it, although it was only a mile and a half away from where she lived. She couldn't even picture in her mind what it looked like.

"What about the girls?" Margaret asked suddenly, trying to remember the names. Brenda was the oldest, she thought. The baby was … Natalie. Nancy. She just couldn't remember.

"The baby sitter took them into the basement," Maureen said. "But like I said, there was no damage to the house."

Margaret stood quietly with the telephone in her hand, looking at the wallpaper on the wall above the telephone stand. She followed the movement of the designs on the paper from floor to ceiling. Little gray diamonds set against a pale pink background. Floor to ceiling, in perfect rows. Wall to wall in a dizzying movement.

"Mark said that there's twelve dead, so far," Maureen remarked. "And one little girl is missing."

"A little girl missing?" Margaret asked.

"Yah," Maureen said. "On the same street as Alice and Kevin."

"She was playing in her sandbox when it hit," Margaret heard Mark say.

"Yah," Maureen said. "Mark said she was playing in her sandbox when the tornado hit."

"And they still haven't found her," Margaret intoned.

"Not yet," Maureen said. "Listen, Hon. I gotta get going here. Mark has to use the phone to call his supervisor. I'll call you later when I find out anything more about Alice and Kevin. OK?"

"OK," Margaret said absently.

"I'm so happy you and the kids are alright."

"Yes," Margaret said in a monotone. "Thank you. Goodbye."

She hung up the phone and turned back into the kitchen, where her son and daughter were seated at the kitchen table, staring at her.

"Thank you, goodbye," Lorlene mimicked her mother and then giggled, holding a hand to her mouth.

3.

"You can do this, can't you, Denny?" she asked as she stepped into her flats.

"I said I can," Dennis said. "How many times do I have to tell you?"

"I can trust you?" Margaret asked her son. "You can take care of your sister for just a little while. Right?'

"Where are you going again?" Denny asked.

"I'm going ..." Margaret caught herself. Where am I going? she thought. She didn't know. There was just suddenly a need in her to go. To go outside the house and just *go*. Never in all her life had she ever felt a feeling like this. She was amazed not only by the emotion, but by the speed with which it had come upon her.

"I'm going over to my cousin's house, to see how her girls are," Margaret said finally.

"Your cousin?" Denny asked.

"Yes, my cousin."

"The one who is with the Lord now?" Dennis asked.

"Yes," Margaret said as she walked into the living room looking for something, although she wasn't certain exactly what it was she was looking for.

"You know, Mom?" Dennis began.

"No, what, Denny," Margaret said as she slipped on her raincoat.

"Jehovah spoke to Job in a windstorm."

"I know that, Denny," Margaret said.

"Maybe," Denny said. "Just maybe, He did the same with your cousin."

"What do you mean?" Margaret asked, suddenly stopping in the middle of the kitchen and looking at her son.

"I'm just saying, maybe He came to her in a windstorm and told her, 'The morning stars sang together and all the sons of God shouted for joy.'"

"Denny, please," Margaret begged.

"Maybe he said to her, 'I made the cloud the garment thereof, and thick darkness a swaddling-band for you, and I said, "Hitherto shalt thou come but no further: and here shalt thy proud waves be stayed."'"

"Denny," Margaret pleaded. "Please. Stop."

"'Who can number the clouds in wisdom?'" the boy continued. "And who can stay the bottles of heaven? Your dust groweth into hardness and the clods cleave fast together.'"

"Denny," Margaret groaned, holding a hand to her forehead. "Enough!"

"Can't you just imagine that, Mom?" the boy said. "Can't you just imagine Him saying that to her?"

"No," Margaret said, pulling out a pink scarf from the pocket of the raincoat. "No, I can't imagine something like that ever happening."

"But that's what happened," the boy persisted.

"Oh, Denny, please," Margaret said as she tied the scarf around her head, knotting it under her chin. "Now please, *please*, Denny, let Lorlene sleep. OK? No shouting at her to obey you, OK?"

"OK," the boy agreed.

"And no waking her up to read the Bible to," Margaret continued.

"But, she needs to hear …" the boy began.

"No!" Margaret commanded. "No waking her up. All right?"

"All right," the boy said.

"All right," Margaret said as she made her way out the door.

4.

She walked three blocks in the half-dark and the rain. All the street lights were either down or simply weren't working, and only her neighborhood had electricity. As she walked, she tried to be careful to avoid broken glass and large pieces of wood scattered over the grass and dirt. At one point, she almost tripped over a torn arm chair, yellow stuffing bleeding from thick tears in its back.

She made her way through a baseball field two blocks from her neighborhood and saw the first signs of the tornado's real destruction. The houses on the other side of the baseball diamond had been leveled and the trees were stripped bare. She made her way down an alley and out onto yet another street, where the pavement was covered with boards and smashed cars. She was amazed as she walked at the randomness of the tornado. Here the neighborhood was leveled. But just on the next street, all the houses were perfectly intact except for shingles ripped from roofs or an occasional broken window.

"Hey, lady!" someone called at her in the half-light. She stopped, breathing heavily, and looked around. Two men wearing yellow civil defense helmets walked toward her in the dark. "What are you doin' out here?" the older, plumper man asked.

"I ..." Margaret stammered. The rain was falling hard now and she felt the cold water running down the front of her neck into her bra.

"You're not supposed to be out here," the younger, thinner man said. "This street is closed."

"Why is it closed?" Margaret asked.

"To prevent looting," the older man replied as though she should know.

"You gotta get out of here," the younger man said.

"I ... I'm looking for my cousin's girls," Margaret finally managed as she stood before the men, shivering.

"There's no girls around here," the older man said.

"Yes," Margaret persisted. "My cousins. Alice and Kevin Handegard." She waited for a reaction from the men at the name, but there was none. "They died."

"Oh," the younger man said. In the half-darkness, the woman could see him look down at the street sadly.

"In the storm," Margaret continued.

"Were they the couple in the car?" the older man asked.

"Yes," Margaret said. "Yes! That was them."

"I saw the car," the older man went on. He then shook his head. "Too bad."

"Like a soup can," the woman said.

"What?" the older man asked.

"That's what I heard it looked like," Margaret said.

"Yah," he said, after thinking about it a moment. "It did. It looked like a crushed soup can."

"I gotta go see the girls," Margaret went on.

"No, lady, there aren't any girls," the younger man said. "Everyone around here has been evacuated. There's no one here."

"No girls?" Margaret repeated, absently.

"No," the younger man said.

"Did they find that little girl who was in the sand box?" Margaret asked.

"Nah," the older man said. "We've been lookin'. Castin' the flashlight here and there. Up in the trees. Under cars. On rooftops. You never know where a tornado'll take someone and put them down, you know. But no. Tomorrow. Tomorrow, when it's light. That's when someone'll find her."

"But for now, lady, you gotta get outta here," the younger man said. "You can't be here. The National Guard's coming in and then they're gonna close down this whole part of town."

"So I can't get through to my cousin's house?" Margaret asked, pointing beyond them.

"Lady," the older man said. "There is no more house if it's over there, where you're pointing. It's all gone. That whole side of town is half-way across Minnesota by now."

"But I heard her house is just fine," Margaret said. "I heard it's still standing."

"No, lady," the older man said. "There's nothing standing over there. It's all gone."

"You gotta go back the way you came," the younger man said.

"Yes," Margaret said. "I will." She turned and then paused. She looked back at the men. "Thank you."

"No problem, lady," the older man said, nodding his flashlight at her.

She turned and slowly made her way back toward her own neighborhood. Faintly, in the distance, she could hear sirens whining. She looked up at the dark sky and saw first one, then another spotlight flare up against the low-hanging clouds. Slowly, they began moving back and forth, merging, then splitting off, then falling back together again as they scanned the clouds overhead.

She had walked about a block before she realized she must have strayed from her return course home. She paused, looked around at the empty street and the dark, lifeless houses around her and tried to regain her sense of direction. The spotlights were coming from downtown, she knew that much. And her house was west of downtown. She knew that, too. Keeping to the right of the spotlights, she made her way through a yard that separated two houses. The grass was covered with boards and shingles and pieces of cloth and paper. She looked into the dark at her feet to see what she stepping on and, at one point, she almost tripped on a twisted piece of tin. But the darkness was on her so completely, she could barely see anything at her feet. It was at that moment that she felt something jab through the bottom of her shoe and pierce the tender underside of her right foot.

"Oh, Christ!" she gasped as she went down onto the ground, writhing in pain. She sank down into a sitting position on a large, wet board and raised her foot. In the dark, she could see the long nail driven into the sole of her shoe. Blood—black as tar—poured over her white calf and was quickly washed away by the steady rain.

"Oh, Christ!" she hissed as she tried to force the nail out. The pain burned through her foot and up the inside of her leg until she felt cold chills on the back of her neck.

Holding her foot, she looked around her. She was sitting in the backyard of a house. A broken, sagging fence separated the yard from the one next door. Just beyond the fence, she thought she could see the baseball field and, beyond that, she could see the lights of her neighborhood, where the electricity hadn't gone out.

"What am I doing here?" she groaned as she fumbled with her foot in the dark, rocking back and forth in pain on the wet board. "What kind of mother am I, leaving the kids alone, after something like this? And for what? I don't even know? What did I hope to find out here?" She started crying as the rain fell, cold and wet, on her head and neck. Her breath caught in her chest and she started heaving as she tried to catch her breath and calm herself. After a moment or two, she wiped the tears from her eyes and tried to stand up.

"Oh, God," she hissed as she stood on her one good foot. She limped two or three steps before she stumbled over something hard and heavy. Again, she went down, this time front first, into a cold puddle of rainwater. The pain burned up her leg and thigh with even more ferociousness then before.

She pulled herself into a sitting position in the puddle and looked around in the dark. Her clothes were now soaked through completely and her wet hair hung, cold and stringy, in her eyes. She untied the heavy wet scarf and let it fall into the puddle beneath her. She inhaled, exhaled and tried again to get up. That's when she noticed what she had just tripped over.

At first, she thought it was a doll. The small white hand almost seemed to glow in the darkness. But when she reached out to touch the hand, she felt her stomach clench. The skin was cold and wet. A board covered most of the girl, and when the woman lifted it, she saw the small, white face, smeared with mud and covered with what looked to the woman like small, black dots.

"Chicken pox," the woman said sadly. She reached out to touch the dots on the girl's still face, but when she did, she felt hard, thick pieces of wood imbedded into the skin.

"Oh, God," she croaked as she reached out and pulled the girl's heavy, limp body close to her. She lifted the girl's head and looked into the face. The little girl's eyes stared back under half-closed lids. Her battered mouth hung open and only a few strands of hair remained on her head.

"The morning stars sang together and all the sons of God shouted for joy," Margaret hummed as she held the girl to her chest. The girl's dirty, wet slacks hung half-way down her bruised legs. Only the torn collar of her blouse remained, still hanging around her neck like a tattered necklace.

"I made the cloud the garment thereof, and thick darkness a swaddling-band for you," Margaret said. She found herself rocking the child on her lap. Although she wanted to cry, to let out a wailing howl, her eyes were dry and stinging.

"Hitherto shalt thou come but no further; and here shalt thy proud waves be stayed," Margaret whispered to the dead girl in her lap.

A low growl of thunder rolled across the sky. White cracks of lightning flashed against the black sky.

"Who can number the clouds in wisdom?" Margaret asked the girl in her arms. "Who can stay the bottles of heaven?"

She traced the soft, cold, heavily pocked outlines of the girl's cheek and let her finger slip down across the smoothly descending line of the jaw.

"Your dust groweth into hardness and the clods cleave fast together," Margaret whispered.

Carefully, with a tenderness she never knew she had before that moment, she rocked the bruised body quietly as she pulled the deeply buried wood splinters from the dead girl's face.

THE DOWNSTAIRS TENANT by Jamie Parsley

"I COULD'VE GONE ON FOREVER"

■

It all happened on a Thursday morning, in April of 1961. Later, that was all Alice Stott would remember. It all happened on a warm spring morning in April. Spring cleaning day for her.

Certain details stood out in her memory when she later thought about the events of that day. She remembered awaking to a cool breeze blowing in through her open bedroom window. She remembered, even years later, the white curtains, bordered with small pink knit flowers, that billowed, that flapped once, twice and then fell back against the window screen like a sail. She lay in bed for several moments watching those curtains rise and fall with the breeze before she got up and started her day. She remembered how, even without her glasses, she watched the movement on the ceiling of the alternating play of half-light and shadow, dancing and swaying there as the curtains rose and fell with the wind.

Other things she did not remember as well. She supposed she must have yawned and stretched her aching muscles. Certainly she let her right arm fall across the empty side of the bed, as she always did. The sheets there were always so cool. The bedspread beside her was smooth and unrumpled. She always turned her head and looked at the pillow across from hers. She always touched it with a tenderness that even made her feel sad. She certainly caressed the wrinkle that creased the linen case where her finger rested.

Certainly she would have whispered to that empty place beside her something like, "Another day. Another day, and another night to follow it."

As she sat up into a sitting position, she groaned a little. She reached out to the bed stand and took her glasses. Slipping them onto her nose, she blinked and tried to focus her eyes.

"Spring cleaning day," she whispered to the empty space in the bed and waited. Silence came back at her, and the sound of the cool breeze in the screen. She swung her feet to the floor and found the slippers there with her toes, slipping her feet into them.

Her son, Luke, usually woke at seven. By that time, when he came down from his bedroom, she had been up for almost an hour. In that hour, she had bathed, dressed and stripped her bed of its sheets. She shucked the pillows of their cases. She stripped the bedspread, leaving only the bare mattress on the box spring. She piled all the sheets into a large wicker laundry hamper and, panting, she wrestled the hamper down to the main floor. There, in the kitchen, she collapsed in her chair at the table to rest a bit. In the kitchen, she tried desperately to regain her breath. She felt a tightness in between her eyebrows and a cold numbness on her arm just underneath her armpit. She slipped off a loafer and touched her ankle with her bare toe, where the skin was swollen. She shook her head, slipped the loafer back on and, taking a deep breath, managed to carry the hamper to the basement, where her new washer and dryer sat in one dark corner. The bare light bulb swung overhead as she fed her bed linens into the gaping black mouth of the washing machine.

As the bedclothes ran their cycle, she climbed the stairs back to the kitchen and quietly made herself a breakfast of two bran muffins and a stout cup of coffee. It was seven fifteen when her son, Luke, finally shuffled into the kitchen, a cowlick sticking straight up from the part in his hair.

"Comb your hair, why don't you?" she commanded. Nothing at that moment bothered her more than the stubborn wedge of hair sticking straight up in the air.

"Why comb it?" Luke mumbled. "I'm gonna be wearing a cap all day."

"Fine, then," she said. She was standing at the sink, washing her breakfast dishes. "Don't comb it. Look like that, then."

"I will, then," he said as he got up from the table and moved past her to the cupboard, from which he took down a box of cereal. She had already laid out the milk bottle on the table, as well as the bowl and silverware.

"Where is it you're working today?" she asked without turning from the sink to face him.

"Mr. Hoag's north field." He was talking with his mouth full of the milky goo of cereal.

Even though she knew the answer, she asked, "By the river?"

Although she couldn't see him, she knew he was nodding. She listened to him munching his cereal.

"Did Kent come out at all yesterday?" she asked.

"No," he mumbled, his mouth full.

She shook her head. "You know, if he can't come out and at least see how you are, then I don't know why you're doing it."

"He needs help," Luke said.

"He needs help. Well, that's nice, isn't it? He needs help. Everyone needs help."

"I know," he said.

"I need help," she said.

"I know."

"Nobody helps me. I could go and have myself a stroke. I could fall right down on this floor, like Kent Hoag, and there would be no one."

"No one," Luke said.

"No one to do your washing. No one to clean this place. No one to make the meals. No one."

She bit her bottom lip to keep from saying anything more. She turned on the faucet and let water run down the drain. She turned the water off and listened to it gurgle in the pipes. Then she started scrubbing at the enamel again.

"He's got some migrants coming next month to help out," Luke said after a while.

"Migrants?" she asked.

"From Texas."

"Christ," she mumbled. "You'll have a great time working with them."

"Mom …," Luke started.

"You better leave your wallet at home, though," she said.

"Mom …"

"Take along only enough money that you can spare to lose," she instructed.

"Mom," Luke said. "I'm not going to be here next month."

She was scrubbing at the little black mark that had always stained the sink's enamel.

"You can't trust those people," she said, making circular motions over the black spot with the rag. "They live different than us, you know."

"I said I'm not gonna be here next month."

She scrubbed at the little black mark harder.

"And don't go listening to their talk, either," she said. "Before you know it, they'll be taking you to Mass with them."

"Mom," Luke said, setting his spoon back into his nearly empty bowl. "I'm leaving. Three weeks from Thursday."

"Oh, you are, are you?" she said, still not turning around.

She heard Luke push the bowl away from him. His chair creaked and she knew he was sitting back in his chair. "Yes, I am."

"Fine," she said. "You go, then."

"Why does it have to be like this?" he asked. "Every time it's like this."

She didn't say a thing as she looked up at the wall above the sink. A calendar hung there. On the calendar was a color photo of two very blond children—a boy and a girl—in a field of bright yellow sunflowers. Beneath the photo, it read: Compliments of Stilson Farmer's Bank, Stilson, North Dakota. Telephone: 526.

"I wish it didn't have to be this way," Luke continued. "I wish …" and then his voice trailed off.

"What?" she asked as he read the caption over and over again to herself. "What is it you wish, Luke?"

"I dunno. I wish maybe you could just give me—I dunno—your blessing, maybe? I wish—I wish to God, I wish!—that you could just be happy for me."

She bit her lower lip, but it didn't help. She threw the wet washcloth into the sink and spun around on her heel.

"Happy is it? You want me to be happy?"

"Yes," he said.

"OK, Luke. I'm happy! I'm overjoyed! Nothing makes me more happy than having you traipse off to school with your little 'pals' and leave me, high and dry, to fend for myself on this farm …"

"I'm not 'traipsing,'" Luke began.

"… the farm your father and I built up to what it is." Mockingly she clasped her hands together. "Oh, Luke! Go! Go and have fun with those filthy-minded punks. Go on. Take the money your father worked for all those years and just blow every last penny on partying and girl-ogling and whatever else it is they do in those big-city colleges. You just go right on ahead, Luke. I'll give you my blessing!"

She waved her hand in the air in a sad Protestant attempt at the sign of the cross. It ended up, however, looking more like a lop-sided diamond traced in the air.

"That's not true," Luke said. He shook his head at her. "You know none of that's true."

"No. Don't *you* tell me what's true or not true here. I *know*. Do you think I've been blind these past few years? Do you think I don't know what you and that pack of hoodlums do when you go to town on the weekends? Oh, I might not see it with my own two eyes. But I know."

"Yah," Luke shot back. "You don't need to use your own two eyes, do you? Not when you have the crowlike eyes of Tessa Nagle."

Alice felt the blood drain from her face. "You listen here! Tessa Nagle doesn't have to be ashamed of one damn thing *she* does! It's too bad *you* can't say the same."

"I think we've already covered this ground," Luke said. "But just to make it crystal clear, Mother, I'll tell you. I have never done one thing wrong. And neither have any of my friends. Yes, we do go to town. You bet we go to the movies. Sure, we talk to girls. So, what's the crime, Mother? You think we should be locked up for it?"

Alice felt her fingers tighten into fists as the anger inside her swelled.

"You do a lot more than that! You drink. I know. I can smell it on your clothes the next morning when I'm washing them. You drag-race on the highways. You've done that right there in front of the Hoag farm. They can see from their windows that it's your car. Selma Hoag brought it up to me one Sunday morning in church. Right there in front of the Episcopal Women's Guild. She told me that if it was anyone else's kid, she would've called the sheriff. You mess around with those sloppy little O'Reilly girls. Right there in the Orion Theater, nonetheless! Tessa saw you. She was sitting three rows back. Right there in the theater, you and that trashy Philomena O'Reilly were licking and fawning all over each other like a pair of filthy animals! Trashy Irish Philomena O'Reilly. Tessa said it looked like you had your hand in her shirt! I didn't want to know where *she* had *her* hand. My God! Don't you think I saw the lipstick stains on your shirt collars when I took them out of the hamper?"

Luke shook in his seat. His face flushed quickly from red to purple with anger. The dark flush of his face only made his blond hair look lighter, almost white. He struggled to speak.

"I'll admit I'm not a saint, like you ..."

"Now, you wait just one minute ..."

"No, Mom. *You* wait! I'll admit I've drank a little ..."

"A little?" Alice said, throwing her hands up in the air and casting a look to the ceiling.

"... and I'll admit I've done things that you don't like. I mean, what exactly do you approve of? But, that's all beside the point. I've never once broken a law ..."

"No. You sure haven't. Underage drinking. No there's no law about that, is there?"

"... I am not going to college because all my friends are," Luke continued. "Out of all those guys, only Billy Tilquist and Roger Peterson are going to college and Roger's already at St. Eric's in Minnesota. Billy's waiting for me to finish up here and then he and I are going to be roommates. We're going to help each other out. You know Billy. He's hung out with me since we were in kindergarten together. You know he's not a 'hoodlum.' He's not going to lead me down the road to ruin."

"Billy Tilquist!" she sneered. "That stupe! What college would ever accept someone as dumb as him?"

"Mom! That's exactly what I'm talking about! Listen to yourself!"

Her eyes narrowed as she gave him a sharp, deep look.

"Mom! You don't have to worry about anything."

"I have plenty to worry about," she hissed. "I don't need *you* to tell me I have nothing to worry about."

"Fine," he said, standing up from the chair. "Fine, then."

"You just go and do your work," she instructed, waving her hand at him dismissingly. He stared back at her, biting his lips until they were thin and colorless.

"I don't need this," he said.

"Well, then, you go ahead and do something about it." She nodded as she said it.

His eyes narrowed. She was amazed as she stared at him how much he looked like her with that look on his face. It made her uneasy. She felt a slight involuntary muscle spasm quiver in her chest and it frightened her. But she kept her composure.

"You know, Mom," he said. His lips were still thin and white. "I think I *will* do something about it."

She laughed, and although she meant it to be a snort of contempt, it somehow lost its bite between the thought of it and the action. It came out of her mouth almost as a heaving gasp.

"What are you gonna do, then?" she asked, frowning.

"Does it even matter? I mean, *now*?" His voice didn't falter once as he said it.

The spasm in her chest quivered even more as the pressure in her body increased. A trickle of cold sweat escaped from her arm pit and ran down her side.

"What *can* you do?" she croaked. "What are *you* able to do?"

"Plenty," he said without a pause. "I've got money."

The word *money* hit her hard.

"You *father's* money."

"*My* money." He jabbed his chest hard. There was hollow sound as the end of his thumb connected with his breast bone.

"Your *father's* money," she hissed.

"*My* money. My name's on the account!" He spaced each word out evenly so there was no confusion.

"You'd do it, too," she shot back. "Wouldn't you? You'd take it. You'd run off with it."

He stood silently without making a move, slipping on a stained baseball cap over his blond hair. He pulled the visor of the cap down low over his eyes, but even in the shadow cast upon his face, she could see his eyes narrowed at her.

"What are you gonna do?" she asked. "Huh? You gonna run? You gonna take off with your buddies when my back's turned? Huh?"

He stared back. His expression remained.

"Oh, I can just see it," she went on. "Luke Co-Ed. Running off to the big city with his dead daddy's money and his dim-witted pals. Yah, the money'll last you a month. That's enough time to find yourself and your buddy a little 'pad' near campus. Maybe you'll get yourself a nice little job at some fast-food restaurant."

As she said them, she found herself desperately trying to stop the words from coming out of her mouth.

"And then what?" she went on. "Where do you go from there? Once the money's gone. Huh? Don't you dare think you're gonna come back here. No way."

"Classes start in four months," he said with little change in his expression.

"So?" She pointed her chin at him from across the room. "Four months is a long time."

"It's enough time to settle in," he said. "It's enough time to get an apartment, a job, make some money. It's enough time to wipe the dirt from this place off once and for all." When he stopped talking, he squeezed his lips so tightly together she swore she could see a smile playing on his mouth.

She was silent. She waited for him to move and for a moment she thought he wouldn't. The thought played for an instant in her mind that he will never move again. Forever they would stand there, frozen, staring each other down. But then, without a warning, he turned and was at the screen door. Before he opened it, she called out.

"What are you going to do?"

He paused at the door but didn't turn back. She looked at his tall, thin back. The straps of his denim overalls hung loose off his lean shoulders.

"What are you going to do?" she repeated.

He looked back at her over his shoulder.

"Who knows?" he said, shrugging his skinny shoulders.

She bit her lower lip. The action made a wet, smacking sound.

"What ..."

He didn't let her finish.

"Who knows," he repeated. He was still looking at her over his shoulder, his hand on the wooden frame of the screen door. "Maybe I *will* go off to the city. Yah." He nodded quietly to himself. "Yah. Maybe Billy and me'll just get in my car and take out all that money in the bank. Maybe by this time tomorrow, we'll be living it up in the city, far, far away from *this*." He sneered as he said the word. "Who knows? Maybe tonight, Billy and me'll be sitting in some big air-conditioned movie theater, with some real friendly big-city girls. And there won't be any Tessa Nagle around to see whose hands are where."

He was smiling his pale, thin grin at her.

"Yup. Who knows," he said.

She opened her mouth to say something. She knew there was nothing to it. Just his name. That's all she had to do. Call his name, the same name she repeated every day for nineteen years. That was all. And yet, she couldn't. And by the time she made a sound—it was a gurgle of escaping air, deep in her throat—he was gone, the screen door slamming shut in its frame behind him. He didn't even seem to leave a shadow behind him on the porch as he walked out into the morning sun.

He's gone. The thought hung, cold and heavy, in her head.

The tractor belched to life and roared for a full minute before it dawned on her that he was not returning. When she stepped to the screen door, a cloud of dust was rising into the clear, warm morning air and the sound of the tractor was dying away quickly down the road.

She stood there looking through the closed screen door until long after the sound of the tractor had died away and the dust had settled. A breeze came up and whispered in the trees around the house. Sparrows fought each other in the bird feeder that hung from one of the trees on the front lawn. Alice frowned, a vee of wrinkles forming between her eyebrows. The muscle spasm in her chest ebbed slowly away. When it was gone completely, she felt weak and shaky.

She turned from the door and snatched up his empty cereal bowl from the table, the spoon clanging loudly against the stoneware surface. A haze settled on her. It was a numbness she didn't even realize had come upon her until she found herself stuffing Luke's bedding into the dryer and discovered she had been working through the better part of the morning with her head in the clouds.

"Oh, my!" she whispered, shaking her head as though she were waking from a fitful nap. "I can't let that boy get me this low. I can't let him have the upper hand."

She walked up the creaking wooden steps from the basement to the kitchen, feeling a pressure build slowly and painfully against the vault of her skull. It was so painful, her eyes watered.

She made her way into the living room, where the letter she had written to her sister, Bernice, the night before lay on the roll-top desk. She looked at the sealed envelope, reading its address to herself. *Estes Park, Colorado.* A longing came up in Alice as she looked at her own handwriting on the envelope. *So far away,* she thought. *So far from all of* this.

As Luke's bedclothes churned in the dryer, she walked the letter out to the mailbox, which was at the end of the long gravel driveway that ran from her house to the highway. As she walked the distance, she tried to enjoy the warm, spring air. It was a little cool on the edges and the wind had a real nip to it, so much so that the skin on her legs became slightly numb by the time she made it to the end of the road. As she laid the letter into the silver metal box and slipped the red metal flag up, she saw, further down the highway, Henry Ostervold's gun-metal blue Ford mail truck moving toward her.

Henry pulled the little pickup onto the shoulder of the highway and stuck his head out of the passenger window.

"Hey there, Alice!" he called.

"Hey there, Henry!" Alice called back. "Some day out, huh?"

"Some day," Henry repeated as she slipped the flag down on the mailbox and took out the letter.

"Some day," Alice said.

"You hear about the Russians?" Henry asked.

"No!" Alice gasped, touching her neck. "What happened?"

"They got a guy up in space?"

"They what?"

"Yah, they shot a guy up in space," he said. "It's in the paper there. And the radio."

As she unfolded the newspaper, she grimaced at the headline which read: RED SPACEMAN SAYS: "I COULD'VE GONE ON FOREVER."

"Oh," Alice stammered, as she quickly folded the paper again.

"You know what his first words in space were?"

"I can't imagine," she said.

"He said, 'I see no God up here.'"

"He said that?" Alice exclaimed.

"That's what he said," Henry said.

Alice shook her head. "What's happening, Henry?"

"Who knows? For all I know, they're probably looking right down at us this minute."

Alice looked up into the sky. Only two small white clouds moved overhead. Beyond them, the sky was a light blue color.

"Estes Park, Colorado," he read aloud as he took the mail from the box. "So, how's Bernice?"

"Oh, you know. She's doing just fine," Alice said as she bent over and looked in the passenger window. "You know she and Jim were here about two weeks ago?"

"No!" Henry said as he handed over Alice's mail, tucked into the folded newspaper.

"Yah," Alice said. "They were here for Easter."

"Well, isn't that something?" Henry said. "I bet you had a great time."

"We did," she said as she took the mail and sorted it. A letter from the bank, a water bill, an electric bill and an envelope addressed to Luke with an embossed return address: STUART COLLEGE. She pursed her lips at the letter and slipped it to the bottom of the pile. She unfolded the paper and read the headline: "Russkie Cosmonaut exclaims: I COULD HAVE GONE ON FOREVER."

"So, Luke's sick today, huh?" Henry said, nodding to the envelope.

"Luke?" Mrs. Stott asked. "No. He's not sick. He's in the Hoag's north field today."

Henry frowned. "The Hoags?"

"Yah. He's been doing some work for them these last few days. Helping out, you know, after Kent had his heart attack last winter. You know those two up-starts of his wouldn't even come back from the city to help out around the farm. So, Luke thought he could make some extra money before getting to work on our own fields."

"You say the Hoags?" Henry asked.

"Yah."

"In their north field?"

"Yah. The one on the other side of the river. You know, back there by the railroad tracks."

"Well, you know I was just there."

"Oh?" Alice said, frowning.

"Yah. And I was talking to Kent."

"What about?" Alice asked. She was clutching the mail tightly in her clenching right hand.

"About Luke. He thought he saw Luke's tractor out in the field."

Alice shrugged. "What about it?"

"He saw the tractor. But not Luke."

Alice suddenly felt the chill on her legs run up the length of her spine.

"Yah. He couldn't figure it out," Henry continued. "The tractor, but no Luke."

"No Luke," Alice repeated absently.

"Yah. He said he's heard Luke talking lately about how he'd like to leave any day now for college. He thought maybe that was the case. But for him to leave the tractor like that and not say anything. Well …"

Alice pressed down on the gravel with her foot so hard she felt her muscles and legs tense to the point of a charley horse. She ignored the pain as she bit absently at the inside of her lower lip. Without another word, she turned away from Henry's car and made her way briskly up the road toward her house with her mail tucked under one arm.

"Alice!" Henry called once, but she didn't turn. He watched her as she crossed her front lawn, heading for a pickup parked in the driveway, and then he shifted into gear and eased back onto the highway toward the Morleys' mailbox a mile and a half away.

Mrs. Stott was half-way to the Hoags before she realized she hadn't shifted out of first gear. The engine of the old pickup growled and wheezed beneath the hood.

"No, no," she hissed as she stepped down on the clutch, the charley horse pain in her leg still burning a knot in her calf. "He didn't do this," she said as she shifted. "He couldn't have done this. Not him. He …"

She spun into the Hoag farmyard, scattering chickens and dust. Kent Hoag stood near the door of the barn, wearing a yellow cap and dark denim bib overalls that cradled his hanging belly.

"Well, there's a sight!" Kent chuckled as Alice stumbled from the pickup. "That beautiful Alice Stott tossing my chickens all over the place like a whirling dervish."

"Where is he?" Alice panted, tossing a strand of gray hair from her eyes.

"He?" Kent asked.

"Luke!" Alice exclaimed.

"Luke? Why, I don't know. I was just about to ask you that same question."

Alice felt the ground give out beneath her feet. She struggled to keep her balance. "Wasn't he here this morning?"

"Well, I heard the tractor come in the yard just as I was finishing breakfast. But you know, it was the darnedest thing."

"What?" Alice asked exasperated.

"When I got out of the house, I didn't hear it anymore. I didn't go out there or anything, but I thought I could see it, there through the trees." He pointed in the direction of a windbreak about a half mile from the farm house. "See, you can see it there. It's still parked out there."

Alice squinted through the trees but couldn't make out the tractor. "What do you think happened?"

Kent shrugged. "He probably took off."

"No." Alice said "He wouldn't do that."

"He's done it before," Kent said.

Alice swallowed hard. "What do you mean, he's done it before?"

"He'll just get up and take off across the field there."

"Across the field?" she asked. She was clasping her hands to her chest and playing with the lace around the breast pocket of her apron.

"Yah. Heading west."

"West," she said, looking around, trying to gain her heading. "West," she repeated again. "Wait a minute. West. West. Over there? Toward the Tilquists, you mean?"

"Yah," Kent pointed over his shoulder. She followed his thumb across the field to a tall, fat silo rising from a thick grove of trees.

"Billy Tilquist?" Alice asked, even though she knew the answer.

"Yah. Billy's one of the boys."

Every last ounce of her breath squeezed from her chest as the now-familiar tightness come upon her again.

"I just don't understand it," Kent continued. "Who leaves their tractor right there in the field like that? Who then runs off God knows where? And why do it without saying anything?"

"Do you think that's what he did today?" Alice asked, pointing to the silo.

"Oh, yah. I bet that's where he is."

"The Tilquists," Alice spat.

With that, Alice staggered toward her pickup.

"I don't know that for sure, though," Kent called out as Alice spun out of the driveway.

As she drove, a series of thoughts passed through her mind. She saw them—Luke and buck-toothed Billy Tilquist—taking off in that beat-up wreck of Billy's. Without a word. They'd just pack up and go. "But first," she said aloud as she approached the Tilquist farm. "First they'll stop at the bank and get that money. Oh, yah. I can just see that. And then off they go to the big city."

She was so intent on what she imagined happening that she missed the Tilquists' driveway and had to turn around on an approach. When she parked in the Tilquists' yard, she stumbled from the pickup, ignoring a large barking collie and walked up to the porch. She hesitated before she pounded on the screen door of the Tilquist house. There was a long pause. Then, Mrs. Tilquist, a short, fat, clean-faced woman with black hair, came to the open door, wiping her small, red hands on her apron. Mrs. Tilquist looked at her and, as she did, Alice saw a quick look of recognition flicker in her eyes. A frown followed, making a deep crease on Mrs. Tilquist's glistening forehead. There was another long pause.

"Mrs. Tilquist!" Alice breathlessly exclaimed. "Hello!"

Mrs. Tilquist nodded. There was another uncomfortable pause.

"I'm Mrs. Stott," Alice blurted, touching her breastbone. "You know me. Yes?"

"Yah," Mrs. Tilquist finally said. "I know who you are." She stood on the other side of the screen door, still wiping her hands. She made no move to open the door.

"I'm Luke's mother."

Mrs. Tilquist nodded.

"Have you seen him?" Alice asked.

"Who?"

"Luke!" Alice said. She was desperately trying to control her voice.

The crease in Mrs. Tilquist's forehead deepened. "No," she said, nodding.

"No!" Alice exclaimed. "You don't know where he is?"

"No," Mrs. Tilquist repeated, this time impatiently.

"So, he and Billy didn't take off this morning?" Alice asked.

"Took off? Took off where?"

"To the city," Alice said. Mrs. Tilquist's eyes fell over Alice quickly and coldly. Alice swallowed a hard, sour lump in her throat. She tried desperately to breathe.

"For the city?" Mrs. Tilquist said. "I, I don't understand what you mean."

"To the city," Alice repeated slowly.

"I don't know what you're talking about," Mrs. Tilquist said. "Billy's out working with his dad right now. Luke hasn't been over all morning."

Alice nodded and didn't know what else to say. She swallowed hard again once more.

After an awkward pause, Alice said," I don't know where he is, then."

"You don't know?" Mrs. Tilquist asked, frowning.

"No," Alice said simply.

Mrs. Tilquist's hard expression softened. She reached for the screen door, her hand on the wooden frame. But she stopped just short of completing the movement of opening it.

"He's not still in the field?" Mrs. Tilquist said.

"No," Alice said, her voice cracking. "Kent said he didn't hear the tractor anymore."

"But maybe …" Mrs. Tilquist began, then stopped. "He could still … be there."

Alice stood on the porch sobbing quietly. A cool breeze was blowing in from the north. She felt it work quickly up the length of her legs. Only when it reached the small of her back did she allow herself to shiver at it.

"No, I …" Alice shook her head. "He wouldn't still be …" Alice turned and looked toward the Hoag farm.

"Are you all right?" Mrs. Tilquist asked through the screen door.

Alice didn't answer. She turned with a dazed, uneven stride and made her way across the front yard toward the Hoag farm.

"Mrs. Stott," Mrs. Tilquist called but Alice had stopped listening. As she walked, she picked up her pace. She left the Tilquists' yard and was now walking across a freshly tilled field toward the windbreak that surrounded the Hoags' north field. She had to go. She had to make sure he was gone and not …

She shook her head and with it went any other thoughts that might upset her. No, she thought. He's off with his buddies. He probably had one of his friends from town meet him out here somewhere. They'll be going into town for the matinee, where he'll paw over one of those filthy Irish girls. That's all. She could already hear what his excuse would be when she confronted him—when she would tell him how she made a scene in front of Mrs. Tilquist like that. How she was forced to go traipsing off across their freshly tilled field to look for him only to find his tractor parked in the middle of the field.

But when she stepped through the windbreak and into the field, she saw that the tractor was not parked in the middle of the field like Kent thought it was. Rather it was stalled against a tree on the farther windbreak, just beneath the railroad track. Its tiller, still attached, lay at an awkward angle behind it. The field itself had only just been worked. The comblike furrows were, for the most part, orderly for one pass. Half-way through the second pass, they veered sharply and then trailed lazily to the point where the tractor stood wedged against the tree. As Alice took in the scene before her, it took her several moments to recognize the object laying in the furrows immediately before they began their haphazard journey to the tree. Squinting, her mind slowly began grasping that what it was she was staring at was Luke's denims overalls.

Why, she thought, would Luke have left his overalls in the middle of a field? Before the thought was completely formed in her mind, she saw the blood. It was soaking through the tears the tiller made in the denim. She stopped.

I don't want to move any closer, she thought. But she couldn't tear her eyes away. She couldn't stop her legs from moving. Whatever aches she felt in her legs earlier that April day were gone now, or simply swallowed up by a white numbness that was slowly working through her body. She walked without thinking. She only stopped when she saw his right hand, palm upward, laying there beside him, the fingernails covered with dark black soil.

They came only after she had been lying there in the field for God only knew how long, howling. Kent was there all of a sudden. And so was Mrs. Tilquist. And vaguely she knew buck-toothed Bill Tilquist was there, too, somewhere, standing off to one side. There were others, too, she knew. But she didn't care who they were. All she knew for certain was that they were trying to get her up, trying to guide her back to one farm or the other, trying to get her away from the mass of flesh and denim over which she had collapsed. But she wouldn't go. She growled at them. She swung at them. She picked up clods of earth and threw them into the air at their encompassing shadows. At first they didn't hear what she was screaming, but slowly the words came through the sound of her anguish, even through the hoarseness of her languished howling.

"Get off!" she was screaming at them. "Get off the furrows! He did them! Look how straight he did them! Get off them! Get off!"

She was still screaming almost twenty minutes later when the sheriff's car bounced across the field, followed soon after by the ambulance. And even then, she didn't stop screaming. She only stopped when her voice completely gave out on her and her strength ebbed away. Her eyes rolled back in their sockets and, before she lost consciousness, she saw the clear, light blue sky above her — empty except for a stray white cloud or two — the sky that only days before held above it a man who looked around at the abyss of space and saw nothing.

THE DOWNSTAIRS TENANT by Jamie Parsley

2

A COLD, COMFORTiNG SILENCE

(Six of Yasunari Kawabata's
Palm-of-the-Hand Stories, retold)

THE DOWNSTAIRS TENANT by Jamie Parsley

JESÚS' ASHES

(*a retelling of the story "God's Bones"*)

■

Roy West, who ran the tractor company, Clarence Iversson, who owned the grain elevator, Tommy Mulligan, who helped win the state basketball championship two weeks before, and Steven Murrow, the barber, all received envelopes from Teresa Costas, the waitress at the Blue Jay Café on Front Street. When they opened the envelopes, the first thing each of them pulled out was the carboned-copied letter.

"I am sending you the ashes of Jesús," the badly typed letter read. "My baby boy died only two days after he was born. He just couldn't do it. He couldn't breathe. He couldn't work up enough strength to just live one more day. I watched as the nurses put the tubes in him and breathed their own breath into his little mouth. Only then did he turn and wheeze something resembling a whine. The day before yesterday—Friday afternoon—he moved his mouth three times and died.

"I don't know who the father was. I couldn't tell from the way he looked. I know for sure he didn't look like me; he was so beautiful. When you hold his ashes in your hands, try to think of his face—a clean, beautiful baby face. Not a mole or a birth mark. Only the chubbiest cheeks I've ever seen and a pair of lips that looked like a carp's. And when he died, his bright blue eyes—the color of marbles—rolled back into the sockets and a little milky blood bubbled at his mouth. Besides that, I can't remember a thing about him. I don't remember how he smelled or what color his hair was. The nurse said he had a long nose that curled up on the end and that his skin was the color of a honeycomb.

"I think—and I might be crazy for thinking this—but I think this baby, in the womb, thought to himself, 'I've got to be born unrecognizable, I just can't resemble anyone.' And when he was born, I think he said to himself, 'Now, I've got to die before I begin to be recognized.'

"All of you—every last one of you—turned your backs when I told you about this. I saw the looks in your eyes. The disgust you felt for me was black as pupils in your blue eyes. Black as night. Not at all like the look each of you had earlier, when I was beautiful in your drunken eyes. Beautiful as a centerfold, one of you told me.

"Young Father Iberra came up to my hospital room, after the baby died, and blessed his little body with holy water. He told me, 'Oh, can't you see? This is Jesús.' I said, 'What do you mean?' and Father Iberra said, 'Look at him. He's beautiful. Can't you see? This is God's child.'

"… & so, I'm sending you my child, Jesús. I couldn't decide which of you I wanted him to resemble. I suppose it doesn't matter now. But maybe, in my sending you his ashes, he can resemble all of you at once."

Along with the letter was a holy card of the Infant Jesús of Atocha and a small plastic envelope filled with a pinch of gray ash.

"What the hell?" Roy West said as he sat at his desk in the tractor company, looking at the letter and inhaling deeply on a cigarette.

"What is that?" Marianne McCullom, his pretty-faced secretary, said as she leaned in the doorway of his office, frowning at the small plastic envelope. "Are those drugs?"

"Don't be ridiculous!" Roy West exclaimed, pushing the envelope as far across his desk away from him as he could before it fell off the edge.

Clarence Iversson shivered at the small envelope and held it up to the light. He could make out an almost opaque piece of bone, about the size of a fingernail clipping, settled at the bottom of the bag.

"Mud," he said as he opened the safe and slipped the letter, the bag of ashes and the holy card into a fireproof box. "Just mud. Not a thing recognizable about it. The way it should be. No punishment if there's no proof of the crime. No punishment."

Before he closed the safe, he took out the receipts from the day before.

Tommy Mulligan had tucked the unread letter into the pocket of his letterman's jacket as he left his parents' home. When he got to the high school, he and some of his friends from the basketball team stood in front of his locker laughing as Tommy read the letter aloud.

"You son-of-a-bitch!" the other boys crowed.

"You just can't keep your pants zipped, can you, you horndog?"

Later at lunch in the high school cafeteria, head cheerleader Susan Friedman slipped onto the seat next to Tommy as he joked with his friends about the letter. She moved her smooth, white thigh against his leg and, feeling the sheaf of ashes in his pocket, smiled a toothy grin at him. Absently, she traced her collarbone with one cold finger until her face flushed the color of a peach.

Steven Murrow slipped the envelope of ashes into the drawer in which he kept his scissors and combs and taped the holy card to the mirror, next to a photo of a model with black hair, cut into an Ivy League.

"Do you know Teresa Costas?" he asked every customer who came in that day.

"The waitress at the Blue Jay Café?' his customers would say. "Oh, sure. Ugly girl. Big teeth. Eyes sunk so deep in her skull you can't tell what color they are. Easy as a swing, I've heard. But nice. Real nice. Yah, I know of her."

"Did you hear about her bastard child dying on her, then?" Steven would say as he ran his fingers through his customers' hair.

"No way! Are you serious? Tell me!"

"Well, she sent me his ashes," Steven said quietly.

"What? No! She didn't!"

"I swear to God!" Steven said, placing one hand on his chest and the other, holding his scissors, in the air. "The *ashes*! Have you ever heard of a crazier thing?"

"I haven't. I honestly never have! But the question is, why *you*?"

"How the hell would I know?" Steven lied as he combed his customers' hair with one hand and cut with the other.

At lunch that day, Roy West slipped into the Blue Jay Café on Front Street. Teresa Costas came to his table with her pad and pencil.

"The special is chicken pot pie," she said.

"What's wrong with you?" Roy asked in a whisper. "You know you really should do something with those ashes. Go on and bury them or something. You're gonna get a lot of people in trouble with their wives, you know."

"How can I bury them?" Teresa asked. "I gave the ashes away to all of you. I don't have a single bone to bury." She stood there, chewing her gum loudly, the pencil just touching the pad. "So?"

"So?" Roy repeated, almost pleading with her.

"So," Teresa said impatiently. "Are you gonna have the special or do you want something else?"

HUSH

(a retelling of the story "Love Suicides")

■

Tuesday afternoon, the woman went out to get the mail and, finding a letter from her husband, she felt her blood run cold.

"Oh, God," the woman said, her voice cracking "Two years he's been gone. Two years in November. That Thanksgiving Day, he looked at me, looked at the turkey dinner I made, bunched up his nose and snarled at me. And left! Not a word for two years. And now — this!"

She looked at the postal bar and saw the letter had been mailed from Tassajara Springs, California.

With trembling fingers, she tore the letter open. Her breath caught in her throat as she read it. He didn't address the letter nor did he date it. It said simply:

"I'm telling you, don't let Kylie play basketball. Do you understand what that does to me, every time she bounces that ball against the pavement in the driveway? Every time the ball hits the side of the house or garage? Do you? I can feel it, even here, in my heart."

Later that day, when her daughter came home from basketball practice, the woman took the ball away from her without a word and threw it into the garbage can under the sink. As the ball fell into the can, the plastic garbage bag inside made a slight rustling sound.

"Why?" the girl cried as she stomped to her room. "Why did you do that to me?"

"Shhh," the woman said. "Don't raise your voice."

A month later, also a Tuesday, another letter arrived from the woman's husband. This time, the post bar read Slater, Wyoming.

"Don't let Kylie wear those tennis shoes to school anymore. Do you understand? Do you realize they make a squealing sound on the floors of the school hallway and I can hear it, even here?"

That day, when her daughter came home from school, the woman told her to take the shoes off at once.

"My shoes?" the girl said. "Why my shoes?"

"Just do it, please," the woman pleaded.

The girl handed over the shoes to her mother, who threw them into the garbage can under the sink. As the shoes tumbled to the bottom of the can, the plastic garbage bag made a whispering sound.

The woman then presented the girl with a pair of brown Hush Puppies she bought earlier that day.

The girl looked at the shoes and cried, "I can't wear these with any of my clothes. They don't match."

"You have to wear them," the woman pleaded. "Please. Put them on."

"And what about basketball?" the girl begged. "I can't play basketball in *these*."

The next morning, the girl refused to get out of bed. She simply curled up under the sheets, crying.

"I can't go to school," the girl said. "Not with those ugly shoes. Everyone will laugh at me!"

"Shhh," the woman said, stroking the girl's hair. "Hush now. There's no need to raise your voice."

Another month passed and, on a Tuesday, another letter arrived. At first, the woman didn't recognize the handwriting. It certainly didn't look like her husband's. For a moment, she thought it looked almost exactly like her father's, but since her father had been dead for almost twelve years, she knew it wasn't his. She opened the envelope and found another letter from her husband. This one read:

"You know that bowl Kylie eats her cereal from, that one with merry-go-round horses on it? Take it away from her. Don't let her eat from it. Don't you understand what it does to me, hearing that spoon scrape against the plastic like that? I can hear it, even here!"

As soon as she finished the letter, the woman went to the cupboard and took down the plastic bowl. She looked at it for a long time before she threw it into the garbage can under the sink. As the bowl fell into the can, the plastic garbage bag made a whispering sound. The woman looked down at her daughter's bowl at the bottom of the can.

"Shhhh, shhhh," she said, imitating the sound of the garbage bag.

She knotted and unknotted her eyebrows and then turned back to the cupboard, taking down her own breakfast bowl, which she also threw into the garbage can. The plastic garbage bag made another whispering sound, only louder and more distinct than before.

"Shhhh, shhhh," she repeated.

She took out her dinner plates and threw them into the garbage can. The bag whispered. She took out all her cups and saucers and threw them in. The bag whispered louder than ever. When the bag was filled, she took another from a roll and filled it with silverware, pots and pans. And as she did, she listened to the plastic bag whisper.

"Shhhhh, shhhh," the woman said as she looked through her house for more things to put into the bag. When she couldn't find anything more, she simply flung herself at the patio door. Her body tumbled through the torn screen and out onto the patio. As she fell through, she heard the screen whisper as her body tore it.

Her daughter came running downstairs and into the kitchen.

"Mom! What happened!" she cried. When she saw her mother lying on the patio, the screen door torn, she cried, "Mom! Are you all right?"

The woman got up from the patio floor.

"What did I say?" the woman asked her daughter. "I said, be quiet, didn't I?" And, without warning, she swung her arm in the air. Her hand connected hard against the girl's face. As it did, the woman noticed that even the girl's skin made a whispering sound.

The next month, on a Tuesday, another letter came, this one with a postal bar from Verona, North Dakota. When the woman saw the postal bar, she exclaimed, "He's near. He's so near I can hear him breathing. I can hear even the blood pulsing in his veins!"

"Stop it! Stop it! Stop it!" The letter read. "Stop making so much noise! Don't you understand? Don't open or close the garage door with the remote control anymore. Don't let the phone ring. Don't turn on the TV anymore. No more alarm clocks, or microwave bells! Nothing! Do you understand? Oh, Christ! Just don't breathe anymore! Both of you! Please! It's driving me crazy!"

"Both of you!" the woman whispered. Cold tears fell from her eyes and spread across her cheeks. She called the girl into the kitchen and made her sit down at the table with her.

"Hush now," the woman told her daughter as she turned on the gas in the stove. "Let's be quiet for a while."

"But, Mom ..." the girl began.

"No, no," the woman said, putting her hand over the girl's mouth. "Hush now. It's time to be quiet."

The gas whispered. It whispered and whispered.

The woman held the girl to her chest and told her, "Hush now. Don't make a sound. Not even a little sound. OK? Shhhhh. Shhhhh."

Later that afternoon, the husband arrived from Verona, North Dakota, after driving for two hours. As he approached the house, he suddenly realized there was silence in his head. A cold, comforting silence. Only a very slight whispering echoed in the back of his mind somewhere. When he opened the door, he found his wife and daughter lying on the kitchen floor, side by side, and the kitchen filled with gas. Without a word, the man got down on the floor between his wife and daughter and listened to the gas whisper to him.

THiS

(a retelling of the story "Mother")

∎

1
Gordon's Diary

Sat. 15th of Mar, 1952
Tonight
I was married.
Afterward
I held her to me.
Her skin was
so soft—
soft
and white
like a flower petal.
So, this is what love is,
I thought to myself:
My mother—
this what she felt like too.
As we laid there
I whispered in her ear
I said to her,
Be a good mother.
Because
you know
I never knew my mother.

2.

Gordon's illness

It was so hot. Even for autumn, it was hot. Lois-Ann stood at the window, watching the rust-colored oak leaves fall on the lawn. Beyond the trees, the wheat fields were all plowed into black furrows.

"Indian summer," she whispered.

Gordon was lying on his stomach on the bed. "What did you say?" he asked.

"I said, it's an Indian summer," Lois-Ann said, turning from the window.

"Is it?" Gordon asked. "Is that what they call it?"

"That's what I always called it," Lois-Ann said. She looked down at Gordon's thin, pale back. The bones of his spine were showing through the skin. She took a bottle of tonic from the bedside table and crawled on top of Gordon, straddling his buttocks. She filled her palm with a coating of lotion. She rubbed her hands together, smearing the cool lotion into her palms and slowly applied it onto his back. She massaged her way down Gordon's bony shoulders, along his spine and then worked outward.

"It looks as though …" Lois-Ann started and then let her voice die away.

"What?" Gordon mumbled into the pillow.

"I don't know," Lois-Ann said. "It just looks to me like your body and whatever it is inside you …"

"Yes?" Gordon said.

"It looks to me almost like they want to die together."

"Die together?" Gordon said into the pillow.

"Well, kind of," Lois-Ann said.

"It's in here, you know," Gordon said without moving.

"I know," Lois-Ann said.

"It's inside me, eating away at me."

"Please," Lois-Ann pleaded. "I don't really want to …"

"No, listen," Gordon insisted. "It's working its way toward my heart. Slowly toward my heart."

"Of course, it is," Lois-Ann said. "I …"

"What do you mean by *that*?" Gordon said, raising his head up from the pillow.

"I mean, it's certainly closer to your heart than I've ever been," Lois-Ann said.

After she said it, they were both silent for a long time. Lois-Ann continued kneading the lotion into Gordon's back, working the muscles with her fingertips. Occasionally, as she used the balls of her palms or applied too much pressure with her fingers, Gordon yelped quietly into the pillow, his body tensing beneath her weight.

"After the first time," Lois-Ann said, finally, after several moments. "When you almost died …"

"Yes?" Gordon said.

"You changed."

"How did I change?" Gordon asked.

"You became selfish. It was always *you* from that point on."

"Me," Gordon said to himself.

"You, you, you," Lois-Ann said. "Like the song. Remember that song?"

"The song?" Gordon mumbled into the pillow. "What song?"

"The Ames Brothers," Lois-Ann said. "*You, You, You.*" She sung it quietly to herself as she worked more lotion into Gordon's back.

You, you, you
There's no one like
You, you, you
You could make my dreams come true
If you say you love me too, she sang.

"I changed, huh?" Gordon said.

"Yes," Lois-Ann said. "I don't know what it was. It seemed to me almost as though I could no longer talk to you anymore. You know what I mean? I couldn't *feel* you. I didn't know how you felt about anything anymore. It was as though whatever it was inside you that was killing you, it closed you off for good from me. It came in between us. Remember how you used to tell me everything when we first met? I knew everything there was to know about you. Your dreams. Your hopes. Everything you had planned for yourself. And then, the most important thing in your life happened to you and you all of a sudden stopped telling me anything. I felt as if you would get up—if you could—and just leave me. Just get up and go, if you had anywhere to go. Just you and—and that thing inside you."

Gordon said. "I wanted to go. I did. If I could've, I would've."

"From me?" she asked.

"Yes."

"Why?" she asked. "

Gordon shook his head. "Three-way suicides are cliché now."

"Three-way suicide!"

"Yes," he said. "Everyone's doing it. I just read about one in the newspaper the other day. The wife found her husband in his lover's arms and killed them both and then put the gun to her own head. It's nothing original. No. So, you see, you dying, it would be a three-way suicide."

"A three-way suicide?" she asked. "I just don't understand."

"Yes," Gordon said. "You, me and …" his voice trailed off.

"Oh," Lois-Ann said. "Yes." She was quiet for a long time. Then she said, "But you know. It would've been all right with me, us dying together. The three of us."

"Oh, God," he mumbled into the pillow. "Shut up. Please. I don't want to talk about this."

"I'm just saying …" she began.

"I know what you're saying," he said. "And I don't want to hear it."

"Without you," she began and then paused. "Without you, I'll be … alone."

She found a bone in his upper back and was massaging it in a circular motion with her thumb until Gordon finally stopped biting the pillow and said, "Please! It hurts!"

"Sorry," she said as she leaned back onto his buttocks and applied more lotion to her palms.

"It's all right," Gordon said.

"Besides," Lois-Ann continued as she gently rubbed the lotion over the small of his back. "Just because your mother got it from your dad and you got it from your mother, doesn't mean I'll get it from you. Right?"

"I suppose," he said. "I didn't think I'd ever get sick with it until I actually did get sick. But then …"

"Then," she said.

"Then, I got it."

"It's all right, though," she said. "Isn't it? I mean, if I should get it."

"What?" Gordon said.

"You know, it would ..."

"Don't even joke about it," Gordon mumbled.

"No, I mean if I got it, then you wouldn't feel you'd have to run away from me."

"No," he said. "God! Do you even hear what you're saying?"

"I know what I'm saying," Lois-Ann said.

"Then, think," Gordon said. "Think about Meryle."

"What about Meryle?" Lois-Ann asked.

"You don't understand," he said. "You don't understand what it's like not to have your mother."

She bit her lip until she tasted blood. "Why do you say that all the time? Why do you have to talk me like that?" she hissed.

"What do you mean?"

"Look at me," she taunted, mimicking his voice. "I'm Gordon and I lost my mother when I was little. Feel sorry for me!"

"I don't say that," Gordon said.

'Yes, you do," Lois-Ann said. "Why do you have to be the martyr in this family? No one else is allowed to know pain except you. You throw it in my face every chance you get. You know, I hate it so much, I'm tempted sometimes to just go and kill my mother. Just to show you!"

He squirmed beneath her and tried to push her off him.

"What are you trying to do, Gordon?"

"Get off me," he said.

"Why?" Lois-Ann taunted.

Gordon managed to turn himself over between her legs. She straddled his lower stomach as she looked him in the face.

"Feel better?" she asked.

"No," Gordon said. "Get off me."

"Not until you tell me, Gordon," Lois-Ann said. "Tell me, what gives you the right?"

"What gives me the right?" he said. "I'll tell you what gives me the right. *This* ..." he jutted his chest toward her. "*This*! This—inside me."

"*That*!" she spat. "Don't throw that at me, flaunting it like that! You know what I think, Gordon? I think you're in love with it!"

He was quiet a moment as he looked up into her eyes. Then, without warning, he said quietly, "Maybe ... I am."

Without even a second thought, she raised her right hand and slapped him hard across the cheek. As she did, she heard him yelp, although the sound came out only as a groan, most of it seeming to have been caught tight in his throat. Then she slapped him again with her left hand. This time her hand connected hard against his mouth and she could feel his teeth under the skin of his lips. His eyes filled with tears, but he didn't move beneath her. When she saw that she had hurt him, she sat back on his lower legs and let him sit up. They looked at each other on the bed for a long time. She was wild-eyed. His mouth was bleeding.

"Jesus," he said, touching his mouth.

"Gordon" she said. "I'm …"

"Don't," he said. "I don't want to hear it."

"All right, Gordon," she said.

"What now?" he asked, looking at the blood on his fingers. "What do you want from me?"

"You know what I want," she said.

"No, I don't," Gordon said.

"You can't keep it to yourself," Lois-Ann said. "You know that."

"Lois-Ann!" Gordon exclaimed, shocked. "What are you saying?"

"Come on, Gordon," she said. "Give it to me."

"No," he said, shaking his head as he tried to move away from her, sliding his legs out from beneath her. "No way. No."

"Damn it, Gordon" she hissed. "You have to. Come on. Give it to me." She motioned to him.

He breathed in and out deeply, trying to control himself. Suddenly, he leapt at her, pushing her off his legs and back on the bed. He then pinned her beneath him. He paused, looking down into her face. She looked up at him and opened her mouth as wide as she could. He looked down at her open mouth and the small, pearl-like teeth in her jaw. She looked up at him with dry, gray eyes.

"Fine," he said. "Is this what you want?" He opened his mouth and showed her his bloody teeth.

"Yesss," she hissed.

"All right," he growled and spat blood and saliva into her waiting, open mouth. She closed her mouth and swallowed loudly. She kept her eyes closed for several moments more. Then, as she looked up at him, she licked her lips.

He was having trouble breathing. Everything inside him had tightened up. But slowly, deep inside him somewhere, he felt comfortable and quiet. He felt the warm quietness spreading slowly but surely through his body. Trying to slow his heaving, he looked down at her body. Her flat torso and thin legs felt bony and lifeless beneath him.

Without a word, he tore open her nightie. She didn't even so much as jerk at the sound of the tearing cloth and popping of buttons. He looked at her face and then down at her breast. Squeezing his lips together, he leaned forward and spat onto her left nipple.

"Don't you ever give this to Meryle!" he said. "Don't ever let him touch this with his mouth again."

And with that, he collapsed, breathing heavily, beside her on the bed.

3.
Her illness

Three years passed and, in those three years, slowly and miraculously, Gordon's health returned. He gained weight, his skin turned a bright pink, and for the first time in his life, he developed a belly. A rim of soft, doughy flesh formed around his middle and sagged over his pants. But as Gordon got better, Lois-Ann lost weight. One day about two years after the incident in the bedroom, she awoke one morning looking pale and tired. Gordon insisted she go to the doctor and a week later, she was diagnosed with his illness.

By February of the following year, the end was near. That morning, outside the hospital room door, Meryle was screaming: "Ma! Ma! Ma!"

"Yes," Lois-Ann managed. "I hear you, Meryle honey. Do you hear me? I'm here."

"Ma! Maaa!"

Meryle was kicking the door with his foot.

"Don't let him in," Lois-Ann said to Gordon. "He can't see me. Not like this."

"God, you're cruel," Gordon said, looking at her with disgust.

She turned away from him and looked at the bedroom window. Snow was falling on the other side of iced-over glass in a thick sheet. She closed her eyes.

"I think this has all happened before," Gordon said. "It's like *deja-vu*. When my Mom died, they wouldn't let me in the hospital room, either. I stood in the hallway and screamed until they took me away."

"It's not *deja vu*," Lois-Ann said. "It's fate."

"God!" he groaned. "Fate! Don't ever use that word again. Fate!" He spat as he said it.

The child was screaming at the door.

"Come on, Meryle," Mrs. Stern, the nurse, could be heard saying outside the door. "Let's go into the living room. OK? I'll a play a game with you. How's that?"

"Noooo!" Meryle screamed as he continued screaming and kicking at the door with his foot.

"Do you remember her?" Lois-Ann asked after the boy finally grew tired of kicking. His cries died away to whimpers outside in the hall.

"Who? My mom?" Gordon said. "No. I don't remember her at all."

"How old were you again?" Lois-Ann asked as she struggled for her breath.

"I was three," he said.

"Three," she said, "The same as Meryle." She gasped once more and then was quiet for a long time. Then, she looked at him and asked, "Do you wish you remembered her?"

"As I get older," Gordon said. "I think I'll probably remember her more and more. I think one day I'll just wake up in the morning and there she'll be. Her face in my mind. That's what I want to remember more than anything. Her face. And the way it felt when you touched it. I would really like to remember that. All I remember for sure was screaming in the hallway of the hospital until they took me away."

"Didn't you see her in the casket?" Lois-Ann asked.

"No," he said. "She was taken away to be cremated."

"If you had seen her in the casket, maybe you'd remember her better."

"I don't think so," he said. "All I'd remember is her dead. A cold, white face in a box—powdered and cold. No."

"What do you remember?" she asked.

""I remember screaming in the hallway of the hospital," he said. 'I screamed and screamed until they took me away."

She frowned as more pain came up into her body. She felt her breath leave her and she struggled just to find the next breath. Then, after recovering, she looked at him again. "It's a shame," she said. "Growing up like we have without religion or God or heaven. I sometimes think something—anything—would help at times like this."

"Like what?" he asked. "Life after death scares me. It frightens me to think of unending existence. No end. No rest. Just going on and on like that. No, thanks."

"It would be a comfort though, wouldn't it?" she said. "It would make all this much easier. To *know* what's going to happen next?"

"Yah," he said. "I suppose it would." He smiled at her as he said it.

She tried to smile, too, but instead she grimaced with pain and closed her eyes. As she waited for the pain to pass, she tried to remember all the trips she and her husband took together. The honeymoon to Idaho, the weekend trips to Lake Superior, the yearly trips to the Pacific coast. Then, she started hallucinating and thought she was flying at a high rate of speed over a field of hollyhocks and chrysanthemums. When she opened her eyes again, she couldn't see very well. She reached out and found her husband's hand. It was big and warm and dry.

"I'm very lucky," Lois-Ann said with barely any voice at all. "I'm lucky to have found you and married you."

"Me, too," Gordon said.

"I don't regret having this," she said. "*This … this.*"

Gordon didn't say a thing. He only squeezed her hand.

"When Meryle grows up, make sure he marries," Lois-Ann said.

"All right," Gordon said.

"I always saw it in your eyes that you suffered," she said. "Before we were married, you suffered a lot."

"I did," he said.

"You worried you'd get what your parents had."

Gordon nodded.

"And you did," Lois-Ann said.

"I know," Gordon said.

"But now …"

"Now? What?" Gordon said.

"Now you're better."

"All better," Gordon said with a shrug.

"It's gone now," Lois-Ann said. "From your eyes, the suffering's gone. I can't see it there anymore."

'It's not there anymore," she said.

"*It,*" he said.

"Yes, *It,*" she said. "And that you'd give it your wife. Didn't you?"

"Yah," he said.

"And you did."

"Jesus, Lois-Ann," Gordon said. "Why are we doing this? Why are we talking like this?"

"And you were afraid your child would get it, too," she said.

"Yah," he said impatiently. "More than anything, I was afraid of that. Why are you saying these things?"

"You didn't give it to him," she said. "And you won't. You know that. And I know that. Not now."

"Lois-Ann, honey," he said, taking her hand in his. "Please. Let's not talk like this. OK?"

"All right," she said, looking toward the window where the snow was falling. For a long time, she watched the snow through the iced-over glass. Then she said, "I *was* happy. I was. What we had was good. It was enough for me. Let him know that, will you? Tell Meryle that I was happy. Really happy. Don't let him suffer any more than he has to. OK?"

"OK," Gordon said.

"Don't let him think that getting married is somehow bad," Lois-Ann said.

"I won't," he said.

"That's all," she said and laid back on the big pillow. And even though she couldn't see it, she knew the snow at the window had stopped falling.

4
Gordon's Diary

Thurs. 9th of Feb, 1956

Tonight
she died.
I held her to me.
Her skin was so soft—
soft and white like a flower petal.
So, I thought,
this is what a woman is.
My mother—
she was a woman, too.
As we laid there
side by side
I whispered in her ear.
I said,
You were a good mother,
You were
because
you knew
I never knew my mother.

THE DOWNSTAIRS TENANT by Jamie Parsley

EARTH

(a retelling of the story "Earth")

■

1.

"And a woman stood there, clothed with the sun. And the moon was under her feet. And on her head, she wore a crown of twelve stars. And, being large with child, she cried out in great pain."

2.

    There were seven churches in the town. Downtown, there were Golgotha United Methodist, First Presbyterian, Holy Innocents' Catholic and St. Andrew's Lutheran, all within blocks of each other. On the south side of town, near the highway, was the Pillar of Fire Assemblies of God Church, and on the north side of town, across the street from the high school, was Holy Redeemer Lutheran Church, Missouri Synod. And on Slocombe Avenue, which ran east and west across the town toward the river, there was St. Paul's-by-the-River Episcopal Church. Although not the largest church in the town by any means, it was by its very appearance impressive nonetheless. Its short, fat, turretlike steeple and high, steep roof, covered in blood-red shingles, could be seen from the river. The facade of the church was built from brick mined and carved in southern Minnesota.
    On the corner stone of the church were engraved the words
SANCTUS PAULUS
A.D.1882.

Beneath this were carved the following words of Saint Bernard:

O vere Dei Nate! Tu mihi pater, tu mihi sponsus, tu mihi anima eras. Nunc orbor Patre. Viduor Sponso, desolor Filio; omnia perdo.

Most parishioners of the church never gave much thought to the cornerstone, and even fewer actually understood what the inscription meant. However, occasionally a visiting Latin student, wanting to practice, translated it as:

O truly begotten son of God, You were a father to me, a son, a husband; You were my soul! Now I have no father, am a widow, a desolate, childless mother. Having lost my only Son, I have lost all!

The interior of the church reflected the high church standards of its first rector, the Reverend George Harold Macguire, who came to the town, just out of seminary, from Wisconsin in the spring of 1880. It was the illustrious Father Macguire who had made the tall, ornate wooden high altar, hiring a local wood-worker who had come to the town from Bavaria in the early spring of 1873. While the church's foundation was still being laid, the woodworker was commissioned to design and carve not only the altar but the reredos behind the altar. To give the reredos his special signature, he carved pine trees and mountains along the borders beneath a particularly gruesome crucifix, a leering skull and two femurs crossed beneath it at the cross's base. On the door of the tabernacle, he had carved an ornate cuckoo, its wings raised upward as though it were praising the Most High. On the rood screen above the sanctuary, the woodworker had carved exquisite flowing edelweiss that framed yet another crucifix, even more gruesome than the one on the high altar.

The church and its woodwork was the envy of the town, and throughout its history, the church was visited by architecture and art students, tourists and clergy of all denominations from as far away as Chicago, New York and London. In 1967, twenty years after Father Macguire died, it was placed on the Register of Historical places.

3.
July 1962

It was in front of St. Paul's-by-the-River Episcopal Church that Leon Latermeier and Pearl Roesler were walking on Slocombe Avenue, oblivious to the treasures held within and oblivious also to the bronze Historical Register sign in front of the church. They were intent, instead, on their trek toward the river. It was a hot summer day and they were both dressed in shorts. Pearl had on a T-shirt. Leon, who wasn't wearing a shirt, had a towel draped around his neck. Pearl was carrying a yellow bathing cap in her hands. As they walked, Leon kept trying to pinch Pearl's buttocks.

"Stop it," Pearl said playfully.

"Make me," Leon chided. He wasn't smiling as he reached out for her with his thumb and forefinger.

"Leon!" the girl whined.

Suddenly Leon stopped and looked at the church on Slocombe Avenue. "You know that church there?" Leon asked, motioning toward it with his chin.

"St Paul's?" the girl asked. "Well, yah. Of course, I do. I was baptized there."

"Can I tell you something about that church?" Leon said.

"Sure," said Pearl.

"Well, it was right here—right here on the sidewalk in front of that church, probably where we're standing right now—that my dad told my mom something that changed her entire life."

Pearl looked at the church and then at Leon's face.

"God!" she said. "You don't know how lucky you are."

He blinked at her. "Lucky?" Leon asked, looking at Pearl with disbelief. "I'm not lucky."

"Yes, Leon, you are," Pearl said.

"Why do you say that I'm lucky?"

"You *are* lucky," Pearl said. "Listen to yourself. Listen to what you're saying. Your *mom* tells you about something terrible your *dad* told her in front of St. Paul's Church."

"Yah," Leon said. "So?"

"So, your *father* told your *mother* something."

"Yah," Leon said. "Something *terrible*."

"Even so," Pearl said. "Terrible or not, he told her some*thing*."

"So what?" Leon said.

"So," Pearl said. "Just having a dad who can say something … God! Leon. You *are* lucky."

Leon was quiet.

"You know, I don't have a dad," Pearl said.

"Yah, I know," Leon said.

"I would do anything to have a dad who would say something to me or my mother. Even something terrible," Pearl said. "I used to try to make up a dad for myself. But I couldn't do it. There were so many things I wanted my father to be that I couldn't keep them straight. Sometimes, when I'm really desperate to have a dad, I tell myself that the State Prison is my dad."

Leon, however, wasn't listening to Pearl. He was looking up at the short, brick steeple of the church. His head back, he said, "My father!" He spat the words into the air at the steeple. "You know, I don't even look like him."

"You don't," Pearl said, reaching up and touching his jaw. "But you don't look like your mom, either."

"Yah. That's true," Leon said as kept on looking at the top of the steeple. "I wonder why that is?"

4.
May 1946

"Noooo," Leon's father, Marcus Latermeier, said when his wife, Brenda, announced that she was pregnant with the boy. He had stopped walking and was shaking his head at her violently. "I know it's not mine."

"What?" Brenda asked, astonished. "What are you saying?"

"I'm saying it's not my kid," Marcus said.

"It *is*, though," Brenda said. "It's yours."

It was May and they had been walking on Slocombe Avenue in front of St. Paul's-by-the-River Episcopal Church, sixteen years almost to the day before Leon and Pearl would walk there. They had just come from a picnic in the park down by the river's shore. Brenda was holding a checkered flannel blanket and Marcus was carrying a large picnic basket.

"How do I know it's mine?" Leon asked. "It could be anyone's."

Brenda felt everything stand perfectly still. Suddenly, as though a cloud had passed in front of the sun, a gray film seemed to form over her eyes, clouding them and blurring her vision. She blinked and then blinked again, but nothing helped. She felt tears well on the bottoms of her eyelids.

"I don't know what you're talking about," she said as she continued blinking and rubbing her eyes.

"I'm just saying, it could be anyone's."

"Marcus," she said. "I've only been with you. In my entire life, I've only loved with you."

"I don't know that. Not for sure," Marcus said.

Brenda felt her throat close up and her stomach tighten. She wanted to get down on her knees — right there on the sidewalk in front of St. Paul's-by-the-River Episcopal Church — and beg her husband to listen to her, but she couldn't. Her knees locked and she was sure if she did move at that moment, she would lose her balance and fall to the ground, possibly hurting her child and herself in the process. Besides, everything was so blurred in her eyes. She wasn't sure if the ground was even beneath her feet anymore. She swayed slightly to the side, but caught herself.

Without another word, Marcus set the picnic basket down on the sidewalk and walked away from her. Brenda stood in the shadow of the church, wiping the tears from her eyes and listening to his footsteps until they died away.

For six months, as the baby grew inside her, Brenda's sight grew worse and worse until finally Dr. Holt, the town's optometrist, prescribed thick, horn-rimmed eyeglasses, although even they didn't help and she spent most days lying in bed, her eyes watering with blurriness. Finally, in January 1947, Leon was born. The baby was a breech birth and the doctor, who was drunk, had to perform surgery. He ended up cutting too deeply and was unable to stop the bleeding. Although the baby was delivered healthy, for almost a week, no one was certain if Brenda would survive. It was almost a month before she was well enough to leave the hospital. When she did, the first thing she did was go to her husband's house on a farm just outside town to show him his son.

At first he didn't recognize her because of her glasses. But when she held the baby out in front of her, Marcus shook his head and said "No. Go on!

Get outta here with that. I don't wanna see it."

"It's your son!" Brenda said, holding Leon up in front of her.

"It's not mine."

"Yes! Yes it is!" Brenda pleaded.

"Look at it," Marcus said. "It doesn't even look like me."

"No!" Brenda exclaimed. "He does! Look at his eyes. They're your eyes. Look at his hair. I don't have blond hair. You do. It's your hair."

"It's a bastard!" Marcus shouted. "I don't want it in my house!"

The words drove into Brenda's head with the force of a lightning bolt. The baby began crying loudly.

"Do you know? Do you?" she screamed. "Do you know what you're doing to me!"

Clutching Leon to her chest, she stumbled into the living room as the baby continued screaming. There, through her blurred vision, she saw her husband's hunting rifle near the easy chair he sat in when he cleaned it. She put the baby on the floor near the chair and picked up the rifle.

Marcus had followed her into the living room.

"Don't set it down," he said, motioning toward the crying baby. He didn't see she had picked up the rifle because her back was turned to him. "Just take it and go," he said.

Brenda turned on her heel to face him and, squinting through the thick lenses of her glasses, aimed the rifle at him.

"It's your baby, Marcus!" she screamed. "I want you to say it! I want you to say he's your baby!"

Marcus froze. Without saying a word, without turning, he started to move slowly backward into the kitchen.

"Oh, no, Marcus," Brenda said and moved after him. As she did, she tripped on the corner of the coffee table. Her glasses fell from her face and, at the same instant, the gun in her hands went off. The bullet flew through the room and hit Marcus in the stomach. The force of the blast threw him back into the kitchen, where he fell against the kitchen table.

The blue smoke from the gun rose like clouds of incense in the air. In spite of the smoke, Brenda, having fallen to the floor beside her baby, was amazed as her vision cleared. The cloudiness that covered her eyes over the last half-year simply lifted as though the film covering them dried and peeled away. In its place, everything she looked at was so crystal clear, she thought she would cry out with joy. The first thing she saw, standing amid the blue gun smoke, was a mirrorlike image of herself. She was shocked by the image because she was naked, her flesh white and plump, and two giant black snakes slithering slowly over her body. First one, then the other, attached themselves onto each of her breasts with their mouths. They hung there like that, biting at her breasts as her face contorted in pain and anguish. At that moment, the smoke cleared and there was a yellow light streaming down from above. In the light, she saw Jesus standing on a cloud, dressed in a blood-red robe and wearing a bejeweled crown of thorns. He raised a long, gold-handled spear over his head and flung it down toward her. With an explosion of light, it pierced her clean through her, driving into her back, through her body and out her chest between her breasts where the snakes fed. Everything was filled with light and color, and all the anguish she felt at being bitten by the snakes vanished.

At some point, she passed out and, when she awoke, she found herself in the county jail.

Even after he recovered from the shotgun wound to his gut, Marcus refused to forgive his wife. His mother, who hated Brenda with an almost perverse passion, pushed him every step of the way to prosecute Brenda. In fact, when the judge sentenced Brenda to the State Penitentiary, Marcus's mother shouted, "Thank you, Jesus! Thank you!" at the top of her voice.

5.
August 1947

One day, while Brenda was in prison about five months, a thunderstorm passed over the prison. She went to a window and, looking through the bars at the heavy, gray clouds filled with lightning, saw them part suddenly. There, between the split-open clouds, was a bright yellow light, and in the midst of the light, she saw what she could only describe as God! Not the Jesus she had seen before, after she had shot Marcus, in blood-red robes and a crown of thorns. But rather it was God in a dazzling light that filled her with such gladness that welled up from her very core.

6.
October 1947

Not long after Brenda's vision, a woman named Martha Roesler was incarcerated in the prison. One night several months before, Martha had spotted her boyfriend at a roadside bar, dancing too closely with another girl to the song "When the Lights Go Down Low." She waited for him outside all night and, as he stepped out of the bar with his arm around the girl, Martha shot and killed both her boyfriend and the girl with a pistol that had once belonged to her father. Even after they had fallen to the ground, she calmly walked up to each of them, carefully aimed the gun, and shot each of them in the face at point-blank range.

One day Martha and Brenda were talking and the subject of Brenda's child, Leon, came up.

"Oh," Martha said. "I'm so jealous! I wish I could have a child! I wanted to have my boyfriend's baby so bad. I really did. But now, well …" She put her head on Brenda's shoulder and started to cry. "I'm damned," she said. "I really am. This is death to a woman, to put her in prison and never allow her to have a child when she wants one more than anything else."

"Maybe when you get out?" Brenda asked.

"No," Martha said. "I'll be an old woman when I get out. It'll be past my time. No." She started to cry again. "I would do anything to have a child. Anything. I would have anyone's child. It wouldn't even matter whose."

"Really?" Brenda asked.

"Yes," Martha said.

"You know, I can make you have one," Brenda said.

"What?" Martha said, taken aback. "What are you talking about?"

"I can make you have a child," Brenda said.

"No, you can't," Martha said. "You're a woman."

"I promise you this: I'll be out of here in two months. Just wait till I get out. Then, I'll come back and I'll make you have a child."

7.
January 1948

Two months went by and Brenda was released from prison. About a month after her release, she returned to the penitentiary to visit Martha. Brenda held her hand up to the thick wooden divider between them in the visiting room.

"Touch the wood I touch," Brenda instructed.

Martha held her hand to the wood and they sat like that, staring at each other for several moments, not saying a thing to each other, just simply looking at each other. Then, as though she knew something Martha didn't, Brenda smiled.

Two months later, Martha realized, to her own amazement, that she was pregnant.

When the prison authorities found out about the pregnancy, a scandal quickly erupted. Newspaper reporters swarmed to the prison, gathering in droves in front of the main gate. All the newspapers in the state put the story on their front pages with the same banner headline: PRISON INMATE PREGNANT. The rumors swirled and since Martha refused to say who the father was— she told everyone who asked her the same answer, "I just don't know"—everyone at first suspected the guards. However, as the investigation got under way, it soon became clear that all the guards in the women's wing of the prison were women. No men were allowed contact of any sort with the women prisoners. This not only deepened the mystery and but also the media's interest. Soon all the headlines of the local newspapers read: "IS IT A 'MIRACLE' AT THE STATE PEN?" Before long, even the national media began picking up the story.

A month after the story broke, the prison chaplain, Father Henry Delaney, was interviewed one evening by a famous radio broadcaster who traveled to the prison all the way from New York City.

"So, Father Delaney," the news broadcaster asked with a pursed smile. "Tell us your honest opinion. Do *you* think a miracle has occurred under your nose, here in this prison?"

"You mean, do I think it was a white dove came flying through her barred window?" the priest asked.

"Well ... yes," the newsman chuckled. "Do you think it was ... divine intervention?"

"No," Father Delaney said seriously. "I certainly do not. Nor do I think that we are about to witness the birth of Jesus Christ."

"Well, then, who do you think the father is?" the newsman asked.

"If I knew that answer, you wouldn't be here now, would you?" Father Delaney said.

Inevitably, the news soon died down, and in October, Martha gave birth to a baby girl, whom she named Pearl. The baby was quickly taken from her soon after her birth and offered for adoption.

A week after Pearl was born, Martha wrote a long letter to her friend, Brenda, thanking her for helping her make the baby. However, Brenda never responded to the letter, nor did she ever see Martha again.

8.

July 1962

Fourteen years later, Pearl and Leon were walking in front of St. Paul's-by-the-River Church, on their way to the river to go swimming. Although she still lived with her adopted parents, she was allowed to see her mother, Martha, any time she wanted, since Martha had been paroled from prison a month before and was working at a florist shop on Main Street. Leon's father eventually forgave Brenda and they now lived together on the farm outside town.

"So," Leon said as they walked down Slocombe Avenue toward the river. "You still think I'm lucky, huh?"

"You are lucky," Pearl said.

"Yah," Leon said. "Maybe. But … so are you."

"I am?" Pearl said.

"Sure," Leon said. "Even though you never had a dad, one day you'll have a baby."

"Will I?" Pearl asked playfully.

"Sure," Leon said. "And that baby'll have a father."

"I hope so," Pearl said, giggling.

"And that father will know it is his baby and no one else's," Leon said.

Pearl smiled at Leon, nodding. She reached out and touched his shoulder. The skin was hot from the sun where she touched it.

Leon smiled, shrugged off her touch, and again grabbed at her buttocks, trying to pinch her.

"Stop it!" she squealed.

"Make me," Leon said as they jostled each other down Slocombe Avenue toward the river, away from the church, the steeple of which stood dark and cool in the cloudless sky.

9.

"And the serpent spit water from his mouth. As a flood, it came after the woman. He hoped that she might be caused to be carried away by the flood from his mouth. But the earth helped the woman. The earth opened her mouth. She swallowed up the flood water the serpent spit out of his mouth."

BURYING THE ASHES

(*a retelling of the story "Gathering Ashes"*)

■

There was an airport behind the cemetery. As the boy moved through the thick grove of pines that bordered the graveyard, there it was—the runway and the metal Quonsets with small single-engine airplanes parked in front of them.

A warm breeze blew through the pines and onto his face. As it did, he felt the blood smeared from his nose, thick and sticky, covering his cheek and chin. When he looked back behind him, he saw dark droplets on the pine needles, hanging like red sap from the branches. Above him, the wind made a soft sighing sound in the pine needles, even over the purring engines of the airplanes on the runway.

"Damn nose," the boy swore as he saw the blood that covered the fingers he had just touched his nose with. "Damn, damn nose," he repeated as he searched his pants pockets for a handkerchief. Then he remembered—all his handkerchiefs were in the hamper back at the house. All of them because he used them all over the last three days. As the blood continued to trickle from his left nostril, in desperation he took his silk tie and held it to his nose. Still the blood flowed until he thought he couldn't breathe. Finally he laid down on the grass under the trees on his back and held his chin up, pinching the bridge of his nose with the tie. His mother had told him once that when he got a bloody nose, he should hold his head in just that way.

As he laid there in the cool grass beneath the pine trees, he could hear her voice in his head, saying, "Put your head back, Kenny, and put pressure here." As he thought about it, he smiled thinking how funny it was that he remembered this one thing about his mother, but yet he couldn't remember the taste of the cookies she made, or what her favorite color was.

He heard an airplane engine rev its engines and, raising his head, looked toward the runway in time to see a blue and red Piper Cub with the high wings hop and skip along the pavement as it gained speed. In the space of an exhale, it leapt up off the runway into the air. As it circled overhead, its shadow shimmered through the trees toward the boy. As it moved over him, he closed his eyes and felt a coolness ripple across his face.

He soon felt the blood thicken inside his nostril as it clotted. He squeezed the muscles in his face and tried to get rid of the itching feeling that worked its way along the length of his nose.

The bell from the school on the other side of the cemetery rang. And for the first time in his entire life, he wished he was there. He thought, Can you believe that? I actually wished I was in *school!*

He heard the steady hum of children as they shouted and sang to each other like sparrows. He strained toward the sound to see if he could recognize any of the voices, but they just all jumbled together. Underneath their shouting and laughing, he heard a steady, hollow thumping. It took him a while to figure out that it was the sound of someone in the schoolyard bouncing a basketball against the pavement. He laid there in the cool grass and listened to the rhythm of the basketball and continued to wish he was at school instead of in the cemetery.

Or rather he wished he could be in the airplane that had just passed over. He imagined it as it circled through the limitless blue, higher and higher until the blue turned wispy and gray. In his mind, he could see, far below him, the earth with its pine trees and its cemetery and its school were nothing more than distant dark shadows, swallowed up in the stretching landscape.

"Ken! Ken!" The voice seemed to be calling to him from the sky. From miles and miles away, it seemed like she was calling, "Come here, Kenny!"

He rose quickly from the grass and, brushing branches and dirt from his shirt and pants, he made his way quickly back through the pines into the cemetery again.

"Geez Louise!" his aunt Helen exclaimed as he approached her. "Where were you?

"I had to get my bloody nose stopped," he told her.

"Oh, Ken," she groaned as she looked at the blood smeared over his face. She reached out and picked a small pine branch from his hair. "Well, you stay around here now," she said. "You know your grandpa's in heaven now. Act like it, OK? He can see you, you know. He's looking right down from where he's at and he sees you."

She was holding the black plastic urn in her hands and, as she talked, she shifted it. A rustling sound came from inside the box that made the boy feel strange inside. When she was finished scolding him, she turned and joined the half-dozen people who were gathered near the front of the cemetery, just inside the metal gate. At their feet, a small square hole had been dug in the ground. A pile of dark earth was heaped on a board to the side of the grave.

The boy joined the mourners, feeling awkward standing there with his tie bloody and wrinkled and his white shirt dirty from lying on the ground. Even his patent leather shoes hurt because they were too small for his feet.

"It's amazing," his aunt said to no one really except herself, holding the urn up in front of her face. "This is all there is of him."

The boy swallowed hard when she said it. "No!" he wanted to say to her. "He's at home right now, waiting for me to come in the door. He's there right now. And when we're done here, I'm going to go home and tell him about all of this. I should be there now, anyway, looking after him. He'll be there if we go right now. I shouldn't even be here. I don't even know who you are—you fat, ugly woman."

"Look at them," she said to the boy as she uncapped the urn and tilted it toward him. "It's amazing, isn't it? On the Last Day—that Last Great Day—Jesus will come down from the sky and put these ashes back together. Like a jigsaw, He'll put them together. Oh!" Her gaze moved slowly upward to the sky above them.

The boy leaned forward and looked inside the urn. Squinting, he saw nothing but a few handfuls of what looked to him to be chalky gravel and a few small white bones.

It was then that he realized that these were, in fact, *his* bones. Here, in this box, were the bones of his feet, his fingers. Here was the powder of his hair and nose and ears. All of it was mixed together in this plastic container this strange woman held in her pink, chubby hands. But try as he might, his brain just couldn't do it. He said to himself, It was only three days ago when you were ... were *whole*. Your bones were in place. Your feet, your hands, your ribs. Your hair, only three days ago, was hair, not dust. Your ears were ears. Your nose was a nose. And I would go home right now and hold you, Grandpa, if you weren't jumbled all together at this plastic box.

There was a small spray of blue carnations near the head of the grave where the large headstone read AASLAND. To the boy, they looked artificial against the green grass. It looked to him almost as if someone had dipped them into a sink of blue-colored water and hung them up to drip-dry. They had a kind of streaked color. Yet, try as he might, he couldn't take his eyes off them.

The boy thought, They kind of remind me of what I saw *that* day. He thought, How could I tell anyone about *that*, Grandpa? Who would understand? I don't even understand. But *that* day, when I was alone with you in the hospital room, one minute you were there on the bed and the next—well, the next minute you weren't there anymore. You were hovering near the window, long and thin and blue like a gas flame. Just hovering there, waving back and forth on the air drifts. The boy swallowed hard. He thought, And all I wanted to do was cry. I wanted to reach out and touch you. And then, when the nurse came in, you waved around in the air and ducked out the closed window. And then you were gone. And then the stink filled the room and she told me to go outside and wait in the lounge. And all I did was sit there and cry and wish you would come back for me to take me with you. That you would help me be a blue flame, flying here and there. Like you. But you didn't come back. Instead, *she* came. And everything got so much worse.

The minister—an ornery-looking guy, tall and skinny, with a red stole draped over his shoulders—stepped forward. He carried a thick, green book under his arm. He looked around at the mourners, only glancing at the boy, and then he looked at his watch. He squinted at the boy's aunt and said, "Should we begin? It's eleven."

The boy's aunt nodded and the minister opened the green book. As he started reading Bible passages, the boy's attention drifted. He was suddenly very aware of the sound of the children in the schoolyard nearby. Above him in the trees, the sparrows started singing. They sang and sang until they drowned out the minister's voice and the playing children. The boy looked and, through the trees, he could see the blue sky overhead.

After the Bible readings, the boy's aunt stepped forward and set the urn into the hole. The boy thought, They listened to you, Grandpa. They dug the hole in your mother's grave. Just like you said. More than once I heard you say it. "Bury my ashes in my mother's grave," you said. And they did, because the other day I asked the funeral director to make sure they did it. And even though *she* raised a huffed, I said, "That's what he wanted. That's what he told me." And they did it.

On the other side of the massive headstone, the boy could see a small, flat stone. Under it lay his grandma's urn. There was still fresh dirt around the stone because it had just been set in place a few days before. Next to it lay another slightly older stone, beneath which lay the urns of the boy's mother and father and sister.

The boy stepped forward and looked down into the small shaft. The hole was deep. He'd never seen a hole for ashes that deep and, in his fourteen years, he had seen his share of graves. The grave was so dark that he couldn't see the black urn at the bottom.

When the minister finished his prayers, everyone gathered around the hole responded with "Amen." Then the minister closed the book and invited every one present to take a handful of dirt from the mound and drop it into the grave. The boy's aunt was first. The boy watched as she stepped forward in her expensive high-heeled shoes, almost tripping as she bent awkwardly and picked up a handful of the dirt. She dropped it into the grave and then she took out a handkerchief to wipe the dirt from her hands. She then motioned for the boy. He took the dirt from the pile. It was cool and wet in his palm. He walked up to the grave and let it drop into the hole. It made a hollow, thudding sound against the urn.

"Say goodbye, now, Ken," his aunt said as she put her arm around his neck and squeezed.

But the boy couldn't. He was tired of saying goodbye. He couldn't say a thing. His throat was dry and sore. And since the blood in his nose had dried, he was having trouble breathing. He merely shook his head and, shrugging off her hand from his shoulder, turned away from the grave.

Everyone, except for the boy, walked away and gathered by their cars on the dirt trail that wound its way through the cemetery. After everyone had left the gravesite, an old man in overalls soon approached. He picked up a shovel and took some dirt from the pile. Before he dropped it into the grave, he looked down into the hole. As everyone stood around talking by their cars about how good the boy's grandfather had been, how noble he was in his last sickness, how strong he'd been after losing his wife, and his daughter, son-in-law and granddaughter, all of them within a year, the boy watched the old man fill the small grave in, occasionally packing the dirt with his foot, until the earth reached the top. He then took a square of green sod and placed it over the hole. When he was done, he took a metal plate with two short spikes on it and placed it over the sod. As a final touch, he took the spray of blue carnations and set them next to the metal plate. When he left, the boy walked over to the grave and looked at the metal plate. There it was, his grandfather's name, his birthday and his death, all written on it with removable bronze letters:

SAMUEL L. AASLAND
1899-1964

He then heard someone behind him whisper: "And what about Kenny? What's going to happen to him now?" Then they were all silent for a moment.

The boy ignored the question. He turned his attention instead to the steady hum of another airplane. It was so loud it drowned out the sound of the children in the schoolyard and the sparrows in the trees overhead. The boy looked toward the line of pines at the rear of the cemetery and saw a small red and white plane ascend into the sky. It glided over the cemetery and then ascended even higher. As he stood at the fresh grave of his grandfather, he watched the airplane for as long he could before it disappeared into the seemingly endless blue sky above him.

MAGENTA

(*a retelling of the story "Makeup"*)

■

There were three windows in the apartment Niall fell in love with that spring afternoon. The large window in the living room looked out on a sprawling, wooded park across a quiet street from the apartment building, as did a smaller window in the bedroom. The even smaller window in the bathroom was divided in half by a metal sill. The bottom pane was painted milk white so that one could neither look out of it, nor could anyone look in. The top half was clear. Venetian blinds had been installed above the window by a previous tenant; the white string that unrolled them hung to the side of the window. To look out the window, one had to stand on the toilet. Even then, all one saw was the dark brick building next to the apartment house and the somewhat dank alley that separated the two buildings.

When the landlady first showed the apartment to Simon and Niall, Niall hadn't given much thought to the windows or what they look out onto, or if he did notice, he didn't remember it later. He was, quite simply, too enraptured by the apartment itself. As the landlady pointed out the different features—the wall of glass bricks in the dining area, the hardwood floors in the gigantic living room, the oak beams on the ceiling, Niall bit his tongue to hold back the pleasure he felt for the place.

"So you like it?" Simon asked as they drove back to their minuscule, second-floor walk-up on the other side of town.

"What makes you think that?" Niall said.

"Because you were biting your tongue," Simon said. "I saw the way you were moving your lips. Your mouth's probably bloody by now. And I also saw the look in your eyes."

"Oh, God!" Niall exclaimed. "I love that apartment! Let's get it!"

"We'll sleep on it," Simon said, narrowing his eyes in a mischievous way which Niall knew meant Simon probably wanted the apartment as much as he did.

A month later, after they had moved in, Niall still hadn't even looked out the bathroom window. It was only while he was standing on the toilet to nail a framed lithograph of Joan Miró's *Head of a Woman* to the wall that he glanced out the clear top half of the window. There in the window in the building across alley, he saw a fat woman with a large white hat standing at a sink, dabbing at the corners of her mouth. Putting the frame down on the porcelain toilet tank, he leaned further across the space between the toilet and the window and watched the woman with fascination. As he watched, the woman patted her red hair under the large hat, turned her face this way and that in front of the mirror, puckered her cheeks and turned away, stepping out of his view.

"What building is that?" Niall asked himself. He looked over the dark brick, looking for some sign, some words of some sort that identified the building, but couldn't find any.

He then looked down into the alley. There, he saw a large green Dumpster, filled with flowers. Stenciled onto the side of the Dumpster in white paint, he read RESURRECTION FUNERAL HOME.

"A funeral home," he whispered.

That night, Simon's younger sister, Nancy, came over to help them paint trim on the kitchen cupboards. After they were done, Niall called Nancy and Simon into the bathroom. As they stepped into the dark bathroom, Simon said, "Jesus, Niall! Turn on the light."

"Wait. Just wait a minute" Niall said, as he climbed onto the toilet and the opened the window

After a moment, the almost pungent smells of the flowers dying in the alley below rose through the open window and filled the bathroom.

"What is that smell?" Nancy asked.

"It's flowers," Simon said.

"It's 'mums," Niall said. "You need to look down there, in the alley," he said, motioning to the alley below.

Taking turns standing on the toilet seat, with the bathroom light out and with only the pale orange-colored street light above the back door of the funeral home burning in the alley, Simon and Nancy could all make out the flower displays below them. About twenty of them stood on either side of the Dumspter, some on wire stands, others in Styrofoam vases.

When it was his turn, as he stood there, leaning against the wall beside the window, Simon reached out toward the open pane with his free hand as though he wanted to pick one of the flowers for himself. "It's like a garden down there or something," he said.

"It's like your own little garden of carnations down in the alley way," Nancy said.

"Actually, they're 'mums," Niall corrected again.

It was then that Niall turned on the bathroom light. As soon as he did, Simon saw the gold glitter on the ribbons of the flowers—some reading MOTHER or SISTER or simply BELOVED in cursive— sparkled with the faint light from the bathroom above.

Although he used the flowers as an excuse to look out the window, what Niall really became preoccupied with was the ladies room across the way. From the first time he looked across and saw the fat woman in the white hat, shame burned across his face like a slap. He knew there was something not right in spying on the women, yet, fight it as he might, he could not tear himself away.

Day after day, he watched the women who came into the bathroom—young and old, all invariably dressed in black or dark blue. Only on occasion did a woman come in wearing a bright red dress or a flowery print.

Every day, they would enter—one after the other—and disappear for a few moments into one of the stalls that remained unseen to him. Then, always they would then go to the sink, washing their hands and, checking themselves in the mirror, adjust their make-up.

Young and old the women primped. They patted their hair into place, fingered stray strands beneath their hats, powdered their faces from their compacts and carefully applied their magenta lipstick, usually finishing their regimen by lipping a tissue. Before they left, they looked once more in the mirror, rubbing away any lipstick that might have streaked their teeth.

As he watched them, Niall found himself shivering when he realized that these same lips, only moments before, were being pressed against a cold, pale cheek or the stitched-together lips of a body, laid out only a few feet away in some dark-paneled room unseen by him.

But what amazed him the most was how calm and collected these women were. Never once did he see any of them stand there, alone before the mirror, breaking down or crying. Instead, they calmly applied their make-up as though they were trying to hide their sense of grief behind powder and lipstick. As a result, Niall felt nothing toward any of them, not one ounce of sympathy for those people who could go to a funeral and still show not even the slight sense of sadness at the loss of life.

One day Simon walked into the bathroom and caught Niall leaning on the high sill, his cheek resting on his hand.

"What are you doing?" Simon asked.

Niall jerked away from the window and stood with his back against the wall behind him.

"I'm not … uh …" Niall murmured, unable to find the words. "Nothing"

"You must be doing something," Simon said.

"I'm just … looking at the flowers. Down there in the alley." Niall said this even though he knew the garbage truck had come earlier that afternoon to clear out the displays from around the dumpster.

"Oh?" Simon said frowning. He gently shoved Niall off the toilet seat and then climbed up to take his place. There he looked out the window, glancing first down at the empty alley below. Then, slowly, his gaze rose over the back of the funeral home. Niall didn't know if Simon saw the women in the bathroom, standing over the sink smearing blood-red lipstick on their lips, but when he stepped down from the toilet and looked at Niall, he was nodding. There was no smile, no emotion of any sort on his face. He simply nodded at Niall. "The flowers?" Simon asked.

"Yes," Niall lied.

"All right. So …" He looked at Niall without emotion. "Are you gonna be much longer?"

"Why?" Niall asked as he looked nervously at the floor.

"Why? Because I gotta use it," he said, motioning toward the toilet.

The next day, after Simon went to work and Niall had the apartment all to himself, he was standing at the window gazing without thought into the ladies restroom when he saw, to his shock, a girl come into the bathroom, crying. She was probably in her late teens and, as Niall watched, she stood before the mirror, wiping away the trails of mascara that streaked the corners of her eyes, the sides of nose and her cheeks toward her mouth. Even after she wiped away all the mascara, she still cried and even from across the alleyway, Niall could see the tears glinting in the light. Finally, she gripped the sink and bowed her head, her thin shoulders heaving with sobs beneath her black dress.

Niall stood there, frozen. He was amazed to see someone crying in that room. Never, in all the time he watched those women—those widows, those daughters, those sisters and those friends—did he see one of them cry quite like this—so openly, so unashamedly. It was the first truly honest and genuine display of mourning he'd observed and it made him so uncomfortable he thought his knees were going to give out on him.

Everything he felt toward those seemingly emotionless women was washed away in an instant by the sight of that one sad young girl crying at the bathroom mirror. He felt everything in him tremble as he saw her sobbing, starting in his stomach and working its way up through his body to his face. His eyes welled with tears and his throat tightened. He had to support himself against the wall or his weakened legs would buckle beneath him and he would fall to the floor.

The girl then looked up at herself in the mirror, examining her damp face for a long time. She raised her chin and lowered it, squeezing and then releasing her lips. After several moments of this, she, without any warning, smiled. Her face seemed to unfold the smile which stretched from one side of her mouth to the other. It was so unexpected that Niall felt as though someone threw cold water on him and, before he even knew what he did, he gasped out loud. Although he didn't mean it to be a loud gasp, it *echoed* in the tiled bathroom.

If she would have stayed one moment longer at the mirror, smiling that grin of hers, Niall was sure he would have called out to her. He would have shouted, "Hey, there!" And if she had turned to him after he called out, he would've nodded at her and returned the smile she gave herself in the mirror.

But he never had the chance. The girl turned as suddenly as she smiled and disappeared from the window.

Niall leaned back from his own window and collapsed against the wall, squatting on the toilet beneath him. He looked absently in the mirror across from him at the reflection of the Joan Miró lithograph above his head, breathing deeply, unable to slow his heartbeat.

For a moment he could almost hear Simon's disapproving voice in his head. In that instant, he could almost see the disappointment in Simon's eyes.

"Lord, Niall," he imagined Simon saying to him if he saw Niall reacting this way to that crying teenage girl. "You can't go on like this. This just … this just isn't healthy."

"I know," Niall said aloud. "I know. It isn't healthy."

With his back still to the wall, Niall reached across the space between the toilet and the wall and pulled the string on the Venetian blinds. They fell over the window, shutting out the sight of the funeral home and the alley below, full of dying flowers.

3

THE BISHOP COMES FOR A VISIT

a play

THE DOWNSTAIRS TENANT by Jamie Parsley

THE REV. THOMAS CORROTHERS, *the Rector of Holy Innocents Episcopal Church; middle-aged; medium build*

MYRTLE CORROTHERS, *the Rector's wife, early forties, plump, well-dressed*

BISHOP MILES HULL, *the new Bishop, heavy-set, with wire-rimmed glasses*

Scene: the Rectory of Holy Innocents Episcopal Church; in a small town in rural North Dakota

Time: December 1952

THE DOWNSTAIRS TENANT by Jamie Parsley

PART 1

THE BISHOP:
> [*patting his stomach*]

My! My!

MYRTLE: Full, are we?

THE BISHOP: Full? Let me tell you, Myrtle. That, I may believe, is *the* understatement of 1952!
> [*To* THE RECTOR]

Stuffed, she asks. Yes, Myrtle. I am stuffed. Stuffed, like that poor old duck we just finished off.

MYRTLE: Oh, Miles! You're something else.

THE BISHOP: Quack! Quack!

MYRTLE:
> [*laughing*]

Stop it! I'm going to start crying if you don't stop! Look at me, I'm spilling coffee all over the place.

THE RECTOR: Myrtle! Get ahold of yourself!

MYRTLE: Well, Miles. I'm just happy you enjoyed it. It makes the time I put into it worthwhile.

THE BISHOP: And look at this room!

MYRTLE: Tell me you like it.

THE BISHOP: Myrtle! You've outdone yourself.

MYRTLE: Really? I was worried.

THE BISHOP: Worried? Why?

MYRTLE: I almost didn't get it done on time.

THE BISHOP: In time? Christmas is still almost two weeks away.

MYRTLE: No. Not Christmas. You don't know about the wedding we had in here last Saturday afternoon, then?
 [*To* THE RECTOR]
Thomas! Didn't you tell him about the wedding?

THE RECTOR: Have I been able to get a word in edgewise?

THE BISHOP: A wedding? In here?

MYRTLE: Yes! Right here. See where I'm standing?

THE BISHOP: Yes.

MYRTLE: This is where the bride stood. Beautiful little thing. Not even out of high school yet.

THE RECTOR: Myrtle. Don't start.

MYRTLE: Am I starting anything? Am I, Miles?

THE BISHOP: I don't know. Are you?

MYRTLE: *I* don't think I'm starting anything.

THE RECTOR: Myrtle. Not with company.

MYRTLE:
   [*ignoring him*]
And the groom stood here. A handsome young boy. He was a quarterback on the football team at the high school just last year. And Thomas stood here …

THE BISHOP: Do I take it to understand there's a reason why the service didn't take place in the sanctuary?

MYRTLE: Nothing gets past you, now does it, Miles?

THE BISHOP: That duck certainly didn't, now did he?

MYRTLE: Miles. Miles. Miles. You wicked thing!
   [*She winks at him*]
The wedding was a … how shall we say it? …

THE RECTOR: Myrtle …

MYRTLE: Let's put it this way. The bride wore a very nice *off-blue* suit.

THE RECTOR: I'm not going to tell you again.

MYRTLE: The waist had to be let out just a bit. If you know what I mean.

THE RECTOR: That's enough …

THE BISHOP: I think I get the picture.

MYRTLE: I knew you would. Yes, it was all very nice, though. Hopefully, a day to be remembered by all involved.

THE BISHOP: We can only hope.
> [*He turns toward the china hutch, atop which are several pine boughs wired together*]

That pine garland smells just wonderful.

MYRTLE: Yes! Don't they? It really adds something to the …
> [*in an effected French accent*]

ambience of the room, don't you think?

THE BISHOP: Yes. It really does. It's very … Christmassy.

MYRTLE: I went to the cemetery last week and cut them myself.

THE BISHOP: The cemetery?

MYRTLE: I had to trudge through four feet of snow. But I got them. I couldn't get that sticky … what is it? Sap?

THE BISHOP: Yes, pine has sap. Yes.

MYRTLE: I couldn't get it off my fingers for days afterward.
> [*She looks at her fingers*]

Everything I touched struck to me. It was embarrassing. But it was worth it. I mean — that smell!

THE BISHOP: You said you went to the cemetery for the pines?

MYRTLE: Oh, yes. There's a beautiful pine bush on the Michaels' plot. A big, fat bush right over the grave of one of their boys.
> [*To her husband*]

You know the one.

THE RECTOR: I don't remember.

MYRTLE: Of course, you do. You buried him, for heaven's sake!
> [*She looks at* THE BISHOP *and shakes her head*]

THE RECTOR: One of the Michaels' boys? When was that?

MYRTLE: Oh, it must've been … ten years ago. In Fargo. His mother was at the grocery and he ran out into the street and was struck by a car.

THE RECTOR: Oh … yes. I remember now.

MYRTLE: What was his name? Dotson?
   [*She pauses for a moment; she strokes her chin as she thinks*]
It was Dotson, wasn't it?

THE RECTOR: I don't remember.

MYRTLE: Anyway … I just walked out there with a pair of scissors and — Snip! Snip! -- cut off a bucket of boughs. Just like that.

THE BISHOP: Well, it is a beautiful room. Which brings me back to the subject we discussed over dinner. I can't possibly see how we could look into moving you to a new rectory. I really can't. This house is beautiful.

THE RECTOR: But, Miles …

THE BISHOP: Thomas, let me finish this thought. There are clergy in this diocese who live in houses that are little more than shacks.

THE RECTOR: Yes. I know

MYRTLE: We both know.

THE BISHOP: In the seven months I've been bishop of this diocese, you don't realize how many complaints I get about leaking roofs. Crumbling basements. Ants. Rotting wood in the floors, in the walls.

THE RECTOR: We know, Miles. We …

THE BISHOP: This place is a palace compared to what some rectors and their families live in.

THE RECTOR: We lived in those places, Miles. We know.

MYRTLE: Oh, my! Did we live in some of the worst of those places? Remember the summer the grasshoppers came in through hole in the wall?

THE BISHOP: Then you understand why I can't OK a move? And certainly I can't rebuild.

THE RECTOR: I wish you'd reconsider.

THE BISHOP: Reconsider? Thomas, I look around here and, frankly, I'm surprised you would even bring it up. Of course, I haven't been in this diocese that long. However, I have heard only glowing reports about you.

THE RECTOR:
    [*smiling*]
Well … thank you.

MYRTLE: We're not the type to complain. We aren't.

THE BISHOP: And looking at your file, I've found you to be content under whatever circumstances you lived under. And from what I can understand, there were a few terrible places you've served since you were ordained.

MYRTLE: Oh, could I tell you stories …

THE BISHOP: I'm sure. But that's the reason I was shocked when I received your phone call last week asking me to come out, that you wanted to talk about a new parsonage.

MYRTLE: Miles. You don't know the whole story …

THE RECTOR: Myrtle.
[*Wagging his finger at her*]
No. Let's not.

MYRTLE:
[*to* THE RECTOR]
He needs to know. He's going to hear it from someone else if not from us.

THE BISHOP: Hear what from someone else?

THE RECTOR:
[*sipping his coffee*]
It's nothing.

MYRTLE:
[*to* THE RECTOR]
It's not nothing.
[*to* THE BISHOP]
It's not.

THE BISHOP: Then, I wish you would tell me.

THE RECTOR: Really. It's nothing.

THE BISHOP: Obviously it's … it's something. Otherwise …

[*At that moment there is sound of wood creaking; it's following by the sound of shuffling; it starts out slowly at first*]

[THE RECTOR *and* MYRTLE *look at each other*]

THE BISHOP: Is there someone else here?

MYRTLE:
[*nervously; her coffee cup rattles against her platter*]
No. There's no one. Just us.

[*Wood creaks again; the shuffling resumes, louder now*]

THE BISHOP: Are you sure. I swear I …
    [*He sits up suddenly from his chair; spilling his coffee as he does so*]
Oh, my God! Who's …
    [*He takes two steps away from his chair, looking toward the doorway and collapses*]

[*The lights go down; the only sound is the creaking wood and the shuffling*]

PART 2

[LIGHT UP *on* THE RECTOR, *who is standing over* THE BISHOP. MYRTLE *is kneeling on the floor beside* THE BISHOP, *fussing to wipe the spilled coffee from his jacket*]

MYRTLE: I think ... he is ... he's starting to come around.

THE RECTOR: Thank God.

THE BISHOP:
    [*trying to sit up*]
What ... what happened?

MYRTLE: I think you better lie still for a moment.

THE BISHOP: Oh ... what happened to me?

THE RECTOR: You took a fall. A nasty one at that. You whacked your head good on the coffee table there.

THE BISHOP:
    [*sitting up, looking about with a frightened look*]
Who ...

THE RECTOR:
 [*looking about*]
Who?

THE BISHOP: Who was that?

 [MYRTLE *looks up at* THE RECTOR]

THE RECTOR: Who was who?

THE BISHOP: Didn't you see her?

THE RECTOR: Her? I don't …

THE BISHOP: The woman.

MYRTLE: Me? Is that who you're talking about?
 [*To* THE RECTOR]
Oh, my, Thomas. I think he really hurt himself.

THE BISHOP: No. Not you! That woman. She was …
 [*He waves toward the stairs*]
She was standing right there.

THE RECTOR:
 [*following his point*]
There's no one there.

THE BISHOP: Not now. But … I saw her! She was standing right there. At the foot of the stairs.

MYRTLE: Oh, my. Here, let's get you up in the chair.

 [*She and* THE RECTOR *help* THE BISHOP *into the chair*]

MYRTLE: There we go. Are you feeling all right?

THE BISHOP: I'm just ... I've got a headache, but otherwise ...

MYRTLE: Let me get you some water.

THE BISHOP: Yes. That would be good.

   [*As she exits, she gives* THE RECTOR *a pleading look*]

THE BISHOP: I saw her. Clear as ... as my hand right in front of my face, I saw her.

THE RECTOR: Why don't you tell me what she looked like?

THE BISHOP: She had white hair, done up in ... a kind of braid. You know what I mean?

THE RECTOR: I think so.

[MYRTLE *re-enters with a glass of water*]

THE BISHOP: And she was wearing an apron.
   [*Taking the glass of water from* MYRTLE]
Oh. Thank you, Myrtle.
   [*He takes a long drink from it, as he looks toward the stairs*]

MYRTLE: Are you feeling better now?

THE BISHOP: She stood right there. Right there. I ...
   [*He shakes his head and takes another drink of the water*]
You didn't see her?

MYRTLE: No. I didn't.
   [*Pause*]
Well ...

THE BISHOP: Well? What are you ...

THE RECTOR: Myrtle.

THE BISHOP: What are you talking about?

MYRTLE: I didn't see her … this time.

THE BISHOP: This time? Do you mean …

> [MYRTLE *looks at* THE RECTOR *again*]

MYRTLE: Just tell him, Thomas. He knows now. We can't keep on like this.

THE RECTOR:
> [*nodding, he sighs deeply*]
All right. This is the reason we wanted to talk to you, Miles.

THE BISHOP: You saw her, then? Yes?

THE RECTOR: Yes.

THE BISHOP: It wasn't just … just my imagination.

THE RECTOR: No.

MYRTLE: Not at all.

THE RECTOR: We've seen her.

MYRTLE: And heard her.

THE RECTOR: All night long. The shuffling and the creaking around in the hallway upstairs.

MYRTLE: All day long shuffling up and down those stairs.

THE RECTOR: You know, I lead confirmation classes in the room upstairs.

[THE BISHOP *shrugs*]

THE RECTOR: Well, I do. And let me tell you, Miles. It's hard to do it. It's hard to try to keep a stiff upper lip with a group of fourteen-year-olds while there's disembodied shuffling going on right outside the door.

MYRTLE: Occasionally we'll do a wedding in the parlor here. It's hard to do that when the sound of someone walking up and down the stairs keeps interrupting the rite.

THE BISHOP: [*sighing, leans back in his chair*]
So … who is she? Do you know?

[THE RECTOR *and* MRYTLE *look at each other for a moment*]

THE RECTOR: We think so.

MYRTLE: We're almost certain.

THE RECTOR: Myrtle's positive on this one.

THE BISHOP: So … who is she?

THE RECTOR: We think it's …
[*He hesitates*]

MYRTLE: We think it's Prudence Histon.

[*There is a distant thump; all three jump at the sound*]

THE BISHOP:
[*shocked*]
What was that?

THE RECTOR: Her.

THE BISHOP: Prudence?

[*There is another distant thump*]

THE BISHOP: Father Aidan Histon's wife?

[THE RECTOR *and* MYRTLE *nod together*]

THE BISHOP: But … I buried her.

MYRTLE: I know. I know. It doesn't make sense. But, she's been dead now — what is it — five years?

THE RECTOR: Six years.

MYRTLE: She died right here, you know? In the Rectory.

THE BISHOP: I remember it well. Of a heart attack.

THE RECTOR: Yes. She died right there. On those steps.

MYRTLE: She was bringing the laundry upstairs.

THE BISHOP:
    [*in disbelief*]
I … I remember coming out here from Fargo to do the funeral.
    [*To* MYRTLE]
It was a packed house.

MYRTLE: That's what I've heard. We came here not long after …

THE BISHOP:
    [*running a hand through his hair*]
I don't know. I've never heard anything so … You know, when I saw her standing there just now, I thought, "She looks familiar."

THE RECTOR: You understand now. Don't you?

MYRTLE: We need to move.

THE BISHOP:
>[*shaking his head*]
I need … I need to take a moment to think about this.

THE RECTOR: Well, of course.

MYRTLE: I know how crazy it all sounds.

THE BISHOP: So, how long has this been going on?

MYRTLE: Well, it started right away. Right after we moved in.

THE RECTOR: I don't think Father Histon ever had any strange goings-on before that, did he?

THE BISHOP: Not that I ever heard.

MYRTLE: We moved in here about five months after Prudence died.

>[*There is a distant thump at the word "Prudence"*]

THE BISHOP:
>[*startled*]
Was that … *her* again?

>[THE RECTOR *and* MYRTLE *nod*]

[THE BISHOP *sighs loudly*]

MYRTLE: At first, we thought we could ignore it. I mean, it was just shuffling. It was just creaking. That's all it was for years. It was even kind of …

>[*struggles to find the words*]

... unusual, shall we say? In a nice way. Having bizarre little occurrences — it gave the house "character."

THE RECTOR: As for the shuffling up and down the stairs, all we had to do was put a cardboard box at the head of the stairs.

MYRTLE: We'd hear her shuffling up the steps, the wood creaking on the stairs beneath her. But as soon as she got to that box, she would stop. Just like that.

THE RECTOR: And that was fine with us. We were content. It was a fine house and a wonderful parish. We could live with wood moaning on the stair.

MYRTLE: We lived with worse in some of the church housing we've had.

   [*They all chuckle*]

MYRTLE: And we could put up with noises in the night.

THE RECTOR: Or when visitors were here.

MYRTLE: If they asked — sometimes even if they didn't — we'd just say, "Oh, that cat!"

THE BISHOP:
   [*looking around*]
Do you have a cat?

THE RECTOR: Uh ... no.

MYRTLE: We had a cat when we first moved in.
   [*To* THE RECTOR; *sighs*]
But, the poor thing ran away.

THE RECTOR: That cat was petrified every minute it had to spend in this house. It would sit up there on the piano, its hair on end, and shiver and coo. One day, someone …

MYRTLE: … me …

THE RECTOR: … left the door open just a bit and off that cat went. It raced out of here, quick as a flash.

MYRTLE:
  [*to* THE BISHOP]
Could you blame the poor thing?

THE BISHOP: But … you said you could've lived with the sounds.

THE RECTOR: The sounds, yes.

MYRTLE: Even the shadows.

THE BISHOP: The shadows?

MYRTLE: Oh, the shadows! We'd see them moving all the time. Not right in front of us or anything. Just out of the corner of our eyes. I'd walk into a room and there'd be a sudden movement in the corner of the room. There …
  [*she points in a corner*]
… but when you'd look, there was nothing there.

THE RECTOR: Then, things started disappearing.

THE BISHOP: Things? Like what?

MYRTLE: Cookbooks. Ladles. Spoons and forks. I just thought I was getting absent-minded.

THE RECTOR: But then …

MYRTLE:
> [*sighing*]
… then …

THE RECTOR: … then, *she* started appearing.

THE BISHOP: You mean, like she did just now?

THE RECTOR: Yes. And always in some unexpected situation.

MYRTLE: You'd turn a corner too quickly, and there'd she'd be. Just standing there at the foot of the stairs, looking up, with a sad kind of look on her face.

THE RECTOR: Or I'd come up from the basement, and there she would be, standing in the doorway, looking down at me.

MYRTLE: My sister came to stay with us about two weeks ago for Thanksgiving. She said she woke up in the middle of the night and there was this woman …

THE BISHOP: Prudence …

> [*The same distant thump is heard*]

MYRTLE: … Yes, there she was, standing at the foot of the bed, touching my sister's toes. She looked like she was crying, my sister said.
> [*Clicking her tongue*]
Sad. Just … sad.

THE RECTOR: One of the confirmation kids used the bathroom down the hall last Wednesday. Suddenly, she let out a scream. She came running out of the bathroom …

MYRTLE: … her skirt tucked into her underwear …

The Bishop Comes for a Visit (a play)

THE RECTOR: ... screaming and hollering about the old woman she saw in the mirror.

MYRTLE: The poor, poor dear! We couldn't get that girl calmed down.

THE RECTOR: I just called off the class for the night. I ended up having to drive the poor girl home myself. She was shaking all the way home.

MYRTLE: The worst, though, was the wedding last Saturday. The one we were telling you about.

THE BISHOP: What happened?

MYRTLE: *She* was there.

THE BISHOP: At the actual wedding?

MYRTLE: Yes. Standing right there. In the doorway.
   [*She points to it*]

THE BISHOP: Like some kind of bridesmaid.

MYRTLE: Only bluer.

THE RECTOR: And deader.

MYRTLE: It was a shock. Everyone saw her.

THE RECTOR: How do you explain something like that to people? How do you even begin to say, "Well, this our resident ghost."

MYRTLE: You can't just say, "Everyone, this is Prudence Histon ..."

   [*There is another distance thump*]

THE BISHOP:
> [*uncomfortably*]

Oh, my! This is more than I can even … begin to …

MYRTLE:
> [*after a pause*]

And you'd think that would be enough.

THE BISHOP: There's more?

THE RECTOR: There's more …

MYRTLE: Two nights ago, we woke up from a sound sleep by …
> [*She pauses*]

THE RECTOR:
> [*to* MYRTLE]

Just tell him.

MYRTLE:
> [*sighing*]

We woke up to the piano. It was playing.

THE BISHOP: This piano?

MYRTLE: That's the one.

THE RECTOR: *She …*
> [*deliberately not saying her name*]

… taught piano, you know. To the local children.

THE BISHOP: I didn't know that.

MYRTLE: "Angels We Have Heard on High"

THE BISHOP:
> [*shocked*]

"Angels We Have Heard on High"?

MYRTLE: That's what she was playing. "Angels We Have Heard on High." All night long.

THE RECTOR: Over and over again.

MYRTLE: I haven't had a moment's sleep in forty-eight hours. Do you see the bags under my eyes?
> [*She pulls down her lower eye lid to show* THE BISHOP]

It's too much, Bishop!

THE BISHOP:
> [*leans back again in his chair; after a moment, to* THE RECTOR]

Have you tried anything?

THE RECTOR: Tried anything? I don't know what you …

THE BISHOP: Well … have you tried … a rite or ritual over it?

THE RECTOR: An … exorcism?

THE BISHOP: If you want to call it that. But yes …

THE RECTOR: I went around the house after she appeared at the wedding and I said, "Whoever are you" because we're not fully certain it's Prudence …

> [*Another loud thump*]

THE RECTOR: … though we're *almost* certain it's her. I said, "Whoever you are, please leave us be. We're not here to hurt you. But we would like to live here in peace."

THE BISHOP: And … what happened?

THE RECTOR: There was a loud crash!

MYRTLE: A couple of plates in the china hutch there shattered. As though someone grabbed the hutch and shook it.

THE RECTOR: Later I found a cross thrown from the wall of my study. It was broken and shattered on the floor.

MYRTLE: Oh! And tell him about the Prayer Book.

THE RECTOR: Oh, yes. Later I found the Prayer Book my mother brought over from England when she came over had been thrown against the wall of my study.

MYRTLE: There was a dent in the wallpaper where the book hit it.

THE BISHOP:
    [*rubbing his chin as he thinks*]
This is fascinating.

THE RECTOR: Fascinating, maybe. But we just can't go on like this, Miles.

MYRTLE: We live in a constant state of jitters.

THE BISHOP: Yes. You really do. You just can't go on like this.

THE RECTOR: Anything you can do would help.

THE BISHOP: Well, under certain circumstances, a church or rectory can be condemned.

MYRTLE: Condemned?

THE BISHOP: If the building is structurally unsound. If there are infestations of pests. Or if there's been a murder or a suicide on the premises, a church needs to be resconsecrated.

THE RECTOR: But this isn't the same situation, Miles. None of those options cover our particular situation.

THE BISHOP: I know. But, we certainly can't let your vestry know that the reason we're moving you out is because the ghost of a former rector's wife is making life unbearable for you.

THE RECTOR: Of course not.

THE BISHOP: No, we will have to be more … creative. Of course, if we were in England, it could be different. This happens all the time there.
 [*To* MYRTLE]
Strangely, people tend to be more superstitious there and believe these kind of things. Ghosts and creepy crawlies.

 [MYRTLE *nods*]

THE BISHOP: Personally, I would prefer some kind of ritual to deal with this …

 [*Immediately there is a thump, louder than before following by another, then another*]

THE RECTOR: Miles, I don't think …

THE BISHOP: No, I don't think that's an option, either. I think, considering these circumstances, we can be creative in our reasons to move you to a new residence. Leave it to me. I'll think up a reason.

MYRTLE:
 [*sighing in relief*]
My! That would be wonderful!

THE RECTOR: Yes, it really would.

THE BISHOP: Meanwhile, do you have a place you can go?

THE RECTOR: We have actually thought about this.

MYRTLE: We were thinking we could move into the Hotel Stinson, just across from the depot.

THE RECTOR: The owner is a parishioner. It's very comfortable. Very nice.

    [*The shuffling begins again; the sound of creaking wood can be heard*]

MYRTLE:
    [*looking toward the stairs*]
She's going back upstairs again.

THE RECTOR: Or back down.

THE BISHOP:
    [*rising from the couch*]
I think I will take that as my excuse to part.

THE RECTOR: Are you sure you're going to be fine, with that bump on your head and all?

MYRTLE: Let me get you a cold washcloth.

THE BISHOP: No, no. I'm fine. Fine.

MYRTLE:
    [*bringing* THE BISHOP's *coat and hat*]
Miles, we really do appreciate this. We were so afraid you would not believe us.

[*The creaking on the stairs can still be heard*]

THE BISHOP:
[*putting on his coat and hat*]
How couldn't I believe you? I've seen. I've heard. There's no doubt in my mind. I certainly couldn't live here under these circumstances.

THE RECTOR:
[*shaking* THE BISHOP's *hand*]
Thank you, Miles.

MYRTLE:
[*grasping* THE BISHOP's *hand*]
Thank you so much, Bishop! Thank you!

THE BISHOP: It's the least I can do. Blessings on you both. And … on this house.

[*There is a loud thump at this*]

THE BISHOP: Good night. Thank you, Thomas. Myrtle.

[THE BISHOP *exists*; THE RECTOR *and* MYRTLE *stand in the doorway, looking after him*]

MYRTLE: That went differently than I thought. But in the end, it was all good.

THE RECTOR: Indeed! So, do you want to pack now?

MYRTLE: Just enough articles for tonight. Why don't you call Andy Sheldon at the hotel?

[*The creaking continues*]

THE RECTOR: I will. We'll just get the rest of our things tomorrow. But for tonight, it's the hotel.

MYRTLE:
 [*calling to him as he leaves*]
Thomas?

THE RECTOR: Yes?

MYRTLE: I feel for her.

THE RECTOR: For ... *her*?

MYRTLE: Yes. I feel sad for her. Wandering about. Sad. And angry.

THE RECTOR:
 [*after a moment*]
Yes, I do as well.

MYRTLE: I wish there was something I could do. To help her, you know.

THE RECTOR: I think we are, Myrtle. I think we are.

[MYRTLE *nods*]

[LIGHT COMES DOWN *to darkness; there is only the sound of the creaking; in the darkness there is a sense of movement; the sound slowly dies away. It is replaced by the sound of piano music: "Angels We Have Heard on High." The music goes on for some time before it slowly dies away.*]

CURTAIN

JAN 1 9 2015